ECHO

✦◇ To everyone who uses fantasy books to escape reality. ◇✦

✦ *Chapter 1* ✦

Darkness... that's how every life begins. It's not a scary kind of darkness that makes you worry, more of an anticipating kind. The kind of darkness that makes you excited for what happens next.

That's what I was doing waiting, anticipating for the moment when I would force myself out of the darkness. I shifted slightly in my stone nest, the water swirled around me. *Soon...* it whispered. *Soon.*

Siren don't lay eggs they have live young, but the live young aren't finished developing yet, so the parent builds a stone nest around them where the young can safely finish developing until they're ready to shove themselves out into the world.

Soon it will be my turn. My nest was becoming too small for me. When I was first placed in here there was room for me to stretch out. Now I could barely move. I was only able to shift from side to side. *Soon...* the water whispered. *Soon.*

I tried to stretch a little, feeling the rocks scrape against my skin.

Come... I tilted my head.

What? Straining my frill to hear the almost silent

whisper.

Come… NOW.

Filled with the urge to move I writhed trying to shake off the feeling.

Come! Now! Hurry!

I placed my hands on the stone walls, pressing against them. My tail pushed against the rocks. Filled with fear I slammed my shoulder into a large boulder. Feeling it start to give I shoved harder and with a loud WHOMF, the rock fell away and I shot out, tumbling, panicking.

Freedom…

I stopped and drifted to the floor, looking around. My nest was in a largish cave. Dark purple plants grew in patches on the floor around me. I looked back and started. Behind my nest were three identical ones. I swam over to the closest, curious. Suddenly the nest trembled. I jerked back, startled. After a few seconds, a rock fell away and the nest stilled. Something greenish-gray hung out of the hole. Once again curious, I approached it. It was an arm.

I poked it, when it didn't move I poked it again before peering into the nest. I froze, looking at an unseeing eye that stared back at me. A strange, coldness rushed over me, causing my sail to stiffen and raise.

Dead…

I pulled away from the nest, shivering slightly.

What?

He didn't listen quickly enough.

What do you mean?

If you don't come when I call, you die.

Oh, who was he?

Your brother.

Deciding not to fully consider that, I swam over to the other nests.

2

One had collapsed.

Is that one coming? I asked, staring at the nest.

She is long dead.

I turned to the final nest already knowing the answer. And the other one?

She was never alive.

I looked around. I'm the only one.

Yes.

What is my name?

Echo.

What were their names?

Doesn't matter.

Why not?

They're dead.

I want to know.

Time to leave.

Glancing back one last time at my dead siblings I swam towards the cave entrance. A sharp, tangy scent wafted through the water. The smell made my stomach growl, somehow I knew I was hungry. I skirted out of the cave, only to nearly swim into another Síren floating there. I froze, the strange coldness rushing over me again.

Don't be afraid, he won't hurt you. He's been waiting for you.

He was massive. I later learned he was about two tail-lengths long, from his head to the tip of his tail. I also later learned that tail-lengths were a form of measurement. I blinked up at the other Síren. He was an old male, barely glancing at me as he ate. I looked him over, he definitely was no longer in his prime. His pale green scales were scratched and dented, his sail was torn in several places, and his tail fin had a huge bite mark. Even his frill was damaged, the left frill looked as though something had tried to pull it off.

3

I sniffed the water, the tangy scent I'd smelled earlier was coming from the thing the other Síren was eating.

Small scraps of the thing drifted to the ocean floor.

I darted over, caught one, and examined it. My stomach rumbled louder.

Eat it, it's food.

I flicked my frill nervously, putting the scrap in my mouth while eyeing the older male, when he didn't do anything I grabbed and ate some more scraps. When there were no more scraps I waited for him. Tossing aside the remaining carcass he swam off not waiting to see if I came. Swishing my tail frantically I hurried after him.

Voice? Who is he?

Your father.

Does he have a name? Can he hear you?

He can hear me when I speak to him, but he cannot hear me right now. And yes, he has a name.

Really? What is it?

Not now.

Ok.

While we swam I began examining the other Síren, his sail fascinated me. It started at the top of his head, traveled down his back and ended just before his tail-fin. His sail –and frill- was a slightly darker shade of green than his scales. I twisted to look at my own sail, unlike my father, my sail was bright blue, I tried to look at my frill. But it was just out of my sight –which was understandable, since its frill was on the sides of my head–. Even though I couldn't see it, I knew it was the same shade of blue.

Once again curious, I looked at my arms. The skin on them was dark gray, almost black. Around my arm fins there were patches of black scales. I asked the voice about that.

Why does he have scales all over but I only have

4

patches?

Because you are a Hatchling, he is an Elder.

I wanted to know what an Elder was but I didn't want to annoy the voice, so I stayed quiet. Soon we came to a cave. Swimming inside it, I could see that it was bigger than the cave my nest was in.

The Elder pointed at a bed of dark purple seaweed before swimming towards a bigger bed and coiling up to sleep.

Voice?

Yes, Hatchling?

Who are you, and why can I hear you in my head?

I am the Great Mother, Hatchling, Mother of all your kind. I can speak telepathically to all my children.

Teli, tela...

Telepathically, it is a fancy word for speaking by thought.

Can I do that?

No. No Siren has had telepathy in a very long time.

I coiled up on my seaweed bed resting my head on my arm. Good night, Mother.

Good night, Echo.

I woke up the next morning when the Elder swam past me outside. Blinking, I shook myself awake and followed.

After several minutes he slowed down and rested on a large rock peering over at a school of tiny creatures.

I latched on to a smaller rock next to him.

What's for breakfast? I wondered following his line of focus. I looked at the creatures and frowned. What are they?

Suddenly, the Elder shot past me towards the tiny things.

Fascinated, I watched as he chased them down catching and killing a dozen of them before paddling back to the rock, his arms full. Settling on the rock, he looked at me, "Well? What are you waiting for? Go hunt."

Startled, I almost fell off the rock I was perched on, as this was the first time the Elder had spoken to me. Shaking off the shock, I darted after the tiny creatures. After chasing them unsuccessfully for several minutes I returned to the rock, panting. I glanced at the Elder who ignored me. I huffed and flicked my tail in annoyance.

Think it through. I thought. I looked at the Elder again.

He was much bigger than me, which was why he had no trouble catching the tiny things. Chasing the creatures wouldn't work for me since I was smaller and slower.

Something tickled my fingers and I flinched. I looked down to see a small sea serpent nibbling at the seaweed around my hands. I blinked, distracted, and moved a finger slightly. Seeing my finger move, the sea serpent darted away. My gaze remained on my hands, like the rest of me, my hands were a dark gray almost exactly the same as the color of the rock I was sitting on. I smiled, having found a way to catch the tiny things.

I creeped slowly across the ocean floor, looking up from time to time to make sure I was going the right way. Finding a good spot, I coiled myself around a rock and waited. It didn't take long until the speedy things began swimming above me, I waited a few seconds before launching myself off the rock. The creatures didn't see me until it was too late. They scattered as I shot through the middle of the school, grabbing as many as I could.

6

After doing this a couple more times, I swam back to the Elder who was waiting semi-patiently.

Without glancing at me, he grunted an order. "Stay here," and with that, he swam away. I looked down at my small catch of six, whatever they were, I examined one closely.

The tiny creature was about as long as my hand. It didn't seem to have a body, or maybe the roundish part I assumed was its head was its body. Coming from the round head/body was eight tentacles. I poked the creature. It was soft. Its purplish skin easily squished when I poked it. I ate it, realizing it tasted good, I ate the rest. I wondered what they were called.

"Kraken," said a voice. I whipped around as the Elder settled on his rock, holding what looked to be a larger version of the tiny creatures I ate.

"What?" I asked while he quietly began eating his catch.

"It's a Kraken," he said in between bites. "They're large, carnivorous, sea creatures."

I glanced at the school of kraken. "Those ones aren't very big," I pointed out as the Elder ripped off a tentacle and chewed on it.

"Those are baby Kraken," he replied.

I wanted to ask more questions but I sensed the Elder did not want to talk anymore.

After finishing his Kraken the two of us patrolled the border of a large area I later learned was the Elder's territory.

Well, the Elder patrolled. I just followed, staring wide eyed at the world around me.

At some point the Elder stopped and motioned at a very large looking rock called a 'mountain.' He told me my mom, his mate, lived over there. He said that sometimes he could see her in the distance, patrolling her territory, and that maybe if I'm lucky I might see her too. The Elder described her as having beautiful dark blue scales. Apparently I looked a lot like her. I peered out at the mountain, looking for a dark blue Síren. But unfortunately my attempts were in vain. I couldn't see any. The Elder then tapped me on the shoulder and motioned for me to follow him and we continued on patrolling.

Soon we headed back to the cave, the next few months were like this: wake up, hunt Kraken, patrol the border, hunt Kraken, go to sleep.

After a couple years the Elder decided I was old enough and took me to his hunting spot where he hunted large Kraken. After showing me how, he let me try.

The Great Mother spoke to me from time to time, usually commenting on how I was growing, sometimes to teach me about my home planet, Neptune, or even to tell me little things about myself I hadn't known. One such little fact was that I had open gills, which meant that my gills were slightly wider than other Síren gills. Because of my open gills I had a better sense of smell, but also a higher chance of catching gill-rot, a deadly disease that obviously, affected the gills.

As the years went by, I became aware of the fact that I was beginning to feel uncomfortable with the Elder. I also felt the slight urge to leave and explore the world.

These feelings were faint however, but I still mentioned it to the Great Mother.

Ahhh this is normal for a young Síren like you.
Really?
Yes.
Why?
Síren are territorial creatures, of course a youngling

8

like you hasn't quite developed those instincts yet so you only feel uncomfortable being in his territory. When you become a Wanderling you'll have these instincts and you won't want to be here at all.

I'm going to leave, and be on my own?

Yes.

Why?

It is your nature, all wild-born live alone.

When will I be a Wanderling?

You'll know.

-✦-

Other than hunting as well as a bit of natural medicine, the Elder taught me about our species. Most Síren lived out in the wild oceans of Neptune like me and him. However, some lived together in large cities. The Elder had never been to a city, but he had seen one from afar and could vaguely describe it.

"It's not a place for wild-born Síren like us," he said. "The territories are too small, and it's too crowded."

I tilted my head, "Can you hunt there?"

He snorted. "No. Kraken schools don't go anywhere near there."

I tilted my head the opposite way, chittering softly. "Then how do they get food?" I asked.

He shrugged. "Who knows. It doesn't matter anyway. Come, it's time to hunt," he swam towards the hunting spot. I soon forgot about the city Síren and focused on practicing my hunting and fighting skills.

I did end up learning what the Elder's name was, his name was Gillcutter. I'd once called him that to see how it felt. The Elder had been so startled that he lost hold of the kraken he'd been tussling with. I also tried calling him, dad or father. Didn't like those either so I decided to stick with calling him the Elder. It felt less weird.

✦ *Chapter 2* ✦

One day I made a discovery, I had been swimming around the territory when I came across a small cave, I swam inside curious. There was something vaguely familiar about the cave. Just then it hit me. This was the cave I hatched in! I swam around it, noting familiar things such as the four nests, and the thick purple plants growing across the stones. Spotting my nest I swam over to it. Attempting to poke my head in, I was surprised when I couldn't fit inside.

Somehow it hadn't occurred to me before that I was growing. I looked over myself, observing the differences. I was much longer. When I first hatched, I was not even one tail length long. Now I was over a tail length long. Where I was covered in dark gray skin, pure black scales had already started growing in. I rubbed at a scale, even as a youngling my scales were already a bit scuffed up. Of course that was to be expected, I was a wild-born after all. I turned so I could see my tail, sleek and powerful; it accounted for over fifty percent of my length. I glanced curiously at the other nests, if my siblings had survived and hatched with me, they would have grown too.

Suddenly interested in the other nests. I cautiously approached them, reaching out I touched the first one. When it didn't move I peered through the hole.

Empty. I pulled off some of the stones from another nest…empty. Clicking my teeth, I glanced at the final one, the one that was destroyed.

Why are they empty?

Scavengers most likely, such as kraken or sea serpents.

Hm. I placed a hand against a nest, thinking.

What are you thinking about?

I was just trying to picture what the others might have looked like, but one of them was a male right? I don't know what a male youngling looks like.

Ah. Well as a youngling, your brother wouldn't have looked very different than you. However with maturity, he would've changed.

Really? How?

Well, even though you would have been the oldest he would have grown larger than you, as male Síren tend to be slightly larger than females. His voice would've also deepened in pitch. But other than that, he wouldn't have been any different except for his greeting.

Greeting?

Yes, you don't need to worry about interacting with other Síren right now as a youngling, but eventually as a wanderling you will.

I cringed, imagining interacting with another Síren unrelated to me. That sounds scary.

The Great Mother chuckled in my head. *It sounds scary now because you're a youngling so it's instinct to avoid other Síren in order to defend yourself. For a wanderling or an adult however, interactions are a regular occurrence*

Introductions are very important when meeting a Síren for the first time. Unless you're fighting them for

12

territory, then no introductions are needed.

How do I introduce myself?

It's pretty simple. All you need to say is: My name is Echo, daughter of Gillcutter and Thalassa. Try saying that to get a feel for it.

"My name is Echo, daughter of Gillcutter and Thalassa," I whispered. "Who's Thalassa?"

Thalassa is your mother.

Why haven't I met her? I asked.

Síren are very territorial, even with their mates and wanderlings. Unless you plan to challenge her for her territory, you most likely won't meet her as she is unlikely to come and visit Gillcutter while he is raising a youngling.

Why not?

Your father is busy caring for you right now. Thalassa doesn't want to distract him.

Do all male Síren raise the younglings?

No, it is merely a matter of who is more capable. Gillcutter is older and wiser than Thalassa, and his territory is easier to defend from predators. So they decided that he would raise most of the younglings.

Has Thalassa ever raised younglings?

She did one time, Gillcutter was ill and incapable of guarding a nesting cave. So she raised a batch of three. One was killed in the nest, a second was taken when Thalassa turned her back. The last survived, barely. There are many predators in Thalassa's territory, making it very dangerous for a youngling.

I thought quietly for a moment absorbing all of the new information. You said that my brother's greeting would have been different from mine. How would it be different?

He would have said son of Gillcutter and Thalassa instead of daughter.

13

Why include the parents' names?

It helps Síren determine if they are related or not.

Oh.

Realizing I was starting to feel hungry, I left the cave and headed for the hunting spot.

As I grew older I began spending more time on or near the border and less time deeper in the territory. Normally, the Elder ignored me. Normally I ignored the Elder. But today was different. I could sense it. There was a slight ripple in the water behind me, glancing back to find the Elder was quietly drifting there. I sighed. Two Síren couldn't live in one territory together permanently, and I knew despite being his kin, the Elder would not let me back in.

That's why he was here. To make sure I didn't try to sneak back in. The only way I could possibly stay here was if I challenged the Elder and won. I eyed the Elder's strong muscular tail, upper body, and arms. In comparison I looked weak and flimsy. Yeah. No way was that happening.

Our goodbye was short and simple, there were no tears, no hugs –thank the Mother for that.– Not even any final words. Just a simple nod from the Elder. Whether it was a nod of approval, a good-luck-out-there nod, a don't-even-think-about-challanging-me nod, or even a stop-stalling-and-get-your-sorry-tail-out-of-my-territory-already nod.

I nodded back to him and with a flick of my tail, I swam off, never looking back.

After several hours of swimming aimlessly, I decided to take a break. I was getting tired and a bit frustrated that I hadn't found any suitable territory. Spotting a seaweed patch near some glow shrooms, I darted over and flopped down. Sighing, I let my eyes wander as I rested, half asleep. I awoke with an involuntary chirp of alarm. Sitting up I looked around, wondering what had caught the attention of –

and startled– my half-asleep mind. I let my gaze drift. There!

Something sparkled softly in the dim shroom light. I swam over to whatever it was, and found that only a small part of it was exposed, and the rest was buried under seaweed. I carefully dug it up. Realising that it was an egg. I lifted it out of the seaweed, moving closer to a large glow shroom, I held the egg in the light. It was larger than my fist and deep blue in color, with white spots that gleamed in the light. I tapped it gently, wondering what kind of creature it belonged to. I glanced back at the tangled clump of seaweed which was probably its nest. I frowned. Judging by the smell I could tell nothing had been there recently. There was a faint scent of some creature I didn't recognize, and another scent that I did. Kraken, and a big one too. Whatever this egg's parents were, they were probably dead. I looked at the egg sympathetically, Kraken, especially full-grown ones, were notorious nest raiders.

Well, if the egg has no parents, then I guess that makes it mine now. I thought.

Ahh, the typical Siren tendency of finders-keepers.

Not sure what Mother meant; I wove a small basket to carry the egg in. Slipping the handle around my neck, I continued swimming on.

After swimming around unsuccessfully for several more hours, I stopped to rest on a large flat rock, sending a bunch of slither-fish frantically wiggling away. I grabbed one and munched on it absentmindedly. Something was off. My head snapped up as I looked around.

Somewhere another Siren was watching me. I don't know how I knew but I did. I peered around. Whoever it was, was good at hiding. The space around me was wide open with only a few large rocks and some seaweed. I sniffed the water, I thought I smelled another Síren nearby, but the scent disappeared too quickly for me to tell. I scooted to the edge of the rock and peered under it to make sure no one was hiding under there. I'd had an unpleasant experience with a large angry Kraken a couple years ago. I smiled at the memory, the Elder had given me a lesson on fighting later that day.

"Whenever you're fighting someone, swim up above them, no matter the size difference. Whoever's swimming higher has an advantage."

I looked up in time to see a large bright blue Síren lash out at me. Pain exploded across my face. I shrieked and clutched at my face. I head butted the Síren and slashed my claws across its chest.

Something slammed into the back of my head, and I grunted in pain as light flashed behind my eyes, and slumped as darkness rushed in.

The blue Síren reeled back as the Wanderling went limp. He glowered at the other Síren.

"Took your dang sweet time," he snarled.

The other Síren, a duller, paler blue than the first, snorted. "What? Need me to save you from the scary Wanderling?" he snarked.

The blue Síren growled, "Whatever, is this the last one?"

The pale one shrugged. "Don't know, don't care, a dozen should be enough," he grabbed the Wanderling, "Huh never met a black-scaled Síren before."

The blue Síren started heading back towards the city.

"Who cares? Let's go."

The pale one shrugged and swam after him.

Noticing the basket around her neck the pale Síren paused and peered inside, lifting the egg out, "Huh. A hippocampus egg. Not very easy to find one of those in the wild." He put it back in the basket before hurrying to catch up to the blue Síren.

-✦-

I groaned softly. My entire body ached. As I awoke I realized I wasn't out in the ocean anymore. I was laying in some hole, in the floor of a weird white cave.

It's not a natural cave, I thought dimly. Must be hand-made, maybe I'm in the city. The Elder said something about Sírens that lived in the city had hand-carved caves.

Shaking off the slight dizziness I felt, I stared up at the opening of the hole just above my head. Remembering the blue Síren, I tensed up. I slowly poked my head out of the hole, ready to attack. I sniffed the water warily. Not smelling anything dangerous, I crept out and looked around. Where am I? Why am I here?

The cave was about three to four tail lengths wide and five to six tail lengths long, fairly well illuminated by glow shrooms. With two in each corner and a few more scattered throughout the room. A largeish circle on the floor that was a slightly darker color than the rest of the room was on one side of the cave, and a shiny rectangular thing hung on the opposite wall.

I floated above the hole, a woven seaweed-leaf nest had been placed next to it, the egg I'd found was nestled inside. I scooped it up, but nearly dropped it when my right arm gave out.

I hadn't noticed before that there was a wrap on it, which was a very dark brown that camouflaged against my black scales. I considered removing it but decided against it. I looked around the cave one last time before descending down into the hole, feeling too worn out to do anything but close my eyes and dream.

I wandered through the thick seaweed. It was different from what I had grown up with. This was mostly growing straight up instead of spreading out across the ground. I pushed a massive leaf out of my face and a frightened sea serpent wiggled away. I watched it swim off into the thick seaweed and considered going after it but decided not to. I wiggled out finding myself in a clearing, I looked around. The seaweed started to thin to my left, showing where the patch ended. I floated in place. Quietly thinking.

The seaweed patch was very large. Almost as large as a small territory. The patch would grow with time, and I had seen a lot of places in the seaweed where kraken and other prey would likely have their dens among the rocks on the ground. I smiled, while it would take me a while to get used to the new area, but I could manage it.

As I meandered through my new territory, I memorized places and locations in it. As well as gouging deep scratches and scraping my scales on rocks just outside of the seaweed patch, marking that this territory belonged to me. It took a while to find anything to make my den, but after stumbling upon a sea serpent nest, I wove myself a large, sturdy nest with the large leaves of the seaweed. I stared proudly at my work. Weaving was not one of my strongest skills and making something big enough to sleep in was difficult.

I squinted at it. One of the leaves was glowing with a strange purple light. I carefully pulled the leaf out of the

18

nest to examine it. The purple light seemed to dance, slowly spreading. The leaf looked to be crumbling underneath the light. I watched it, mesmerized. The purple light continued spreading and reached my hand.

"OW!" I yelped and dropped the leaf. The purple light hurt! The leaf fluttered down into the nest, and the light spread.

It flooded across the nest, growing onto the plants supporting it. I stared in horror as the light stretched on even more, turning everything it touched to dust. As it spread, I swam frantically trying to escape it. The light was on the ground, reaching up the plants, and then it was on me. I shrieked in pain as a light-covered piece of seaweed wrapped around my tail. I yanked myself away but it was too late, the light had grabbed my tail. Twisting and writhing, I tried to get it off, but still it spread. I clawed at the light, but it only spread to my hands and arms. I screamed as my arm-fins slowly dissolved to dust.

WAKE UP.

✦ *Chapter 3* ✦

My eyes snapped open to the plain white/gray of the hole. Just a dream. I glanced at my arm-fins, they were flared out from my arm muscles being tensed, but there was no purple light. My arm-fins were intact and not being turned to dust. Just a dream. Shuddering, I swam out.

Mother? Was that you? I glanced around the cave warily, I spotted a flicker of movement out of the corner of my eye.

I'm here, Echo.

What was that?

Did your father ever tell you about anything like that?

No.

Hmm.

I swam over to where I saw movement, finding a small kraken I ate it.

Mother?

Beware of fire, Echo.

Fire? What's fire?

But Mother didn't respond.

I wandered around the cave again, I kept finding little kraken hiding everywhere and eating them. Where were they coming from? After catching all the kraken, I decided to check on the egg. Picking it up I carefully checked it for any cracks. I glanced at the nest and started fidgeting with it, adjusting and readjusting the way the leaves were positioned. I sighed, feeling very bored; There was nothing to do in the cave, I flopped down on my back next to the egg's nest, and stared at the ceiling. I knew that lying on your back was dangerous as it gave other creatures a chance to attack you, but at that point I was so bored that if something tried to attack me, at least then I would have something to do.

Nothing attacked me, of course nothing attacked me. I was in a cave. Alone. With no way in or out. I rolled onto my side, away from the egg's nest.

I thought about the seaweed patch in my dream and grumbled, rolling over again.

"I could've had an amazing territory like that," I whined, now rolling around on the ground.

I rolled around, for a few minutes. Grumbling about the blue Síren and generally acting like a youngling having a tantrum. After the few minutes, I flopped on my back and brushed off my scales. I looked around the cave for any witnesses.

Well, I suppose the one, singular good thing about this cave is that no one saw that. My dignity is still intact. I squinted at what looked like a kraken hiding behind a glow shroom on the opposite side of the cave.

As I was squinting at the possible kraken-witness, something gleamed softly in the corner of my eye. I turned to look at the gleaming thing curious of what new object I hadn't noticed before.

It was just the shiny thing reflecting the light of a glow shroom. I blinked at the shiny thing. I didn't actually know what it did. I rolled over and approached it. It doesn't look

21

like anything special, I thought. Is it some weird decoration the city-born use? Just something they hang on their walls?

I stared at the shiny thing, hesitantly I touched it and jerked back.

It didn't do anything.   "Oh, well that was disappointing," I muttered moving closer. Automatically the shiny thing exploded with light and color. I screeched and shot back into the hole. The light faded and the shiny thing turned black again after several minutes. I didn't leave the hole for the rest of the day.

I woke to a loud screeching sound and darted out of the sleeping hole, looking around. A large rectangular hole had opened up the wall opposite the shiny thing. I slowly crept over, and stared at it.

Am I supposed to go in? I thought to myself. Just then a little kraken darted past and I shot after it. For the rest of the day I watched the new hole as I swam around the cave. Always keeping a little distance between me and it. I found a couple things in the cave during my patrol.

One thing was a clump of ice in a far corner, I wasn't sure what to do with it so I tossed it back and forgot about it.

The second thing was that the dark circle on the ground could be pushed down to see a little tunnel that went off to the side. I'd discovered the tunnel completely by accident when I for some reason decided to punch the dark circle. After I punched it, the circle sank down slightly and then rose back up into its original position. I rubbed my now sore fist as I examined the dark circle curiously, I pressed down on the circle as hard as I could. With the dark circle pushed almost completely down a little tunnel was visible. I was pretty sure that was where the kraken had come from, my suspicion was confirmed a second later when a little kraken darted out from the tunnel and smacked into me. I released the circle and it rose back up into its original position.

It probably lowers so that the kraken can come out. Now my hand kind of hurts but I got a snack so it was sort of worth it.

The next morning I awoke to the smell of something new, a faint scent of another Síren was coming from the new hole. I approached the hole warily when something shot out, slamming into me.

Seeing this as an attack I clawed the intruder viciously. We hit the far wall and tumbled apart, I righted myself and assessed the intruder. Just as my nose told me, it was another Síren, although I didn't expect it to be a young one. The Síren hissing at me had white scales and looked no older than the Youngling stage. The other Síren's sail lifted as it arched its back. I hissed angrily in response as we circled each other, both of us assessing the other for weaknesses.

Distantly I could hear a screeching sound just over the sound of the hissing intruder. I felt my sail flare up as I tensed, the other Síren paused slightly. I charged. Tackling it I managed to briefly pin the other Síren down before it wiggled away. I chased the other Síren around the cave a couple times, both of us getting our piece of the other. Soon we stopped, me on one side of the room, the intruder opposite me. We eyed each other warily, we were both too tired to continue. I descended down into the sleeping hole slowly, pulling the egg and its nest down with me. I didn't want to risk the intruder messing with it.

The next few days were like that, the two of us fighting and chasing each other around. The strange hole the other Síren came out of had closed at some point, so the two of us were stuck, neither of us willing or capable of backing down. I peaked out of my sleeping hole. The other Síren was busy trying to catch some tiny kraken, which had at some point appeared in the cave again –I really gotta start paying attention as to when– I'd noticed the intruder wasn't very good at catching them.

I peered out of my hole and watched the new Síren, I hadn't really paid attention before, but I didn't have anything else to do. At first I'd thought that the other Síren was a youngling because it was definitely smaller than me, but now I could tell that all of its scales were grown, meaning it was a wanderling. Which made sense as younglings don't attack other Síren. Due to its smaller size, my guess was that it was probably a female.

I examined her, the new Síren had a short rounded sail in shades of green, as well as bright white scales that appeared unscuffed. I noticed she had some little marks on her forearms.

Are they scars? I wondered, leaning a bit closer. No... not scars. They're odd scales.

The scars were actually some scales that were gray instead of white like the rest.

Strange. Mother told me that most Síren have scales of a solid color. Although there are a few with a lighter colored chest and stomach, it's pretty rare. I didn't think it was possible for a Síren to have just a scattering of different colored scales. I watched as she pounced on a small kraken, and slithered out of the sleeping hole. She looked up to see me approaching her. She gulped down the kraken and watched me. I stopped barely two arm-lengths away, as we

24

stared each other down.

There was a hesitant truce between us, I was stronger than her but couldn't chase her off, she was more agile but couldn't leave since the hole in the wall closed. We circled each other in our repetitive dance. Then stopped, both of us in our unspoken territories in the cave.

We stared at one another, the other Síren swam a little closer and reached out a hand. I blinked, her frill was pricked forward facing me but not flared in aggression. Her sail and arm fins were lowered, not raised in a threat. This was not a fight. I reached out and pressed my hand against hers. This was a greeting.

She smiled. "What's your name? I'm Sáo, daughter of Frostsight and Flickertail." I blinked. Oh right, introductions.

"Echo, daughter of Gillcutter and Thalassa. Why?"

"Well, I might as well know the name of the Síren who's been beating my tail."

I couldn't help but smile a little at that. We didn't speak much after that for the rest of the day.

The next morning when I woke up, I found Sáo already awake and -unsuccessfully- hunting.

"Son of a slug-kisser," she muttered after she missed yet again.

I stretched my tail and joined her. "Problem?" I asked innocently as I easily nabbed a kraken that was swimming past.

"Gggahhh, it's these slime eating kraken! I can't catch them!"

I snorted, "You think catching them in here is hard? Imagine trying to hunt them in the ocean, where they can just swim forever. Didn't your parent ever teach you how to catch kraken?" I asked.

Sáo eyed me, "No? Mum never needed to teach me that."

I blinked dully at her, "Never needed? Kraken is the base of the Síren diet! All wild-born should learn how to hunt it the minute they leave the nest!"

Sáo flicked her tail at me. "Wild-born? Oh I see why you're confused, I'm not a wild-born, I'm a city-born."

"A city-born huh? That explains why you're so small."

She glared at me for a minute before suddenly gasping.

"What?" I asked.

"Oh Mother! Your scales!" Sáo exclaimed, grabbing my arm.

"What's wrong with them?" I asked, tugging my arm away.

"They're so dull! Haven't you ever cleaned or polished them?"

"What? No." I compared them to Sáo's, they really did look dull next to hers.

I racked my brain, I couldn't remember my father or the Great Mother ever telling me about scale polishing.

"Well I suppose that's just city-born behavior, you have to be super shiny and flashy so all the prey can see you coming," I drawled.

"Well, I guess being shiny is one aspect of it, but actually keeping your scales clean can help prevent parasites and infections," Sáo replied.

She swam over to one corner, picked something up and came back. "Here I found this over there yesterday, we city-born use pieces of hard ice to polish our scales." She held it out in offering. I glared at it and turned away.

I glanced back, Sáo had tossed the ice piece closer to me. I grabbed the hard ice and darted away towards the far wall, grumbling about city-born and their shiny scales. Sáo watched me for a moment before turning to do something else. I scrubbed at my scales grumpily. I glanced over at Sáo, she was hunched over something, muttering to herself.

I ignored her and continued polishing my scales. I looked over my arms after I finished. They were so shiny, I hadn't realized how scuffed and gritty my scales had been before I cleaned them. I smiled, it actually felt nice to have all my scales polished and clean. I swam over to Sáo.

"There, are my horrible wildborn scales clean enough for you?"

She laughed, "Yeah, they're ok now. But you missed a spot," she said pointing to my sail.

"What? Where?" I asked, trying to see where she was pointing.

"Just there."

I spun around in circles, "Where? I don't see it?"

Sáo laughed at me, I stopped spinning. I think I just got tricked.

I jumped a little when the Mother started laughing in my head. *You did.*

✦ *Chapter 4* ✦

I carefully slithered out of the sleeping hole. At some point yesterday after the entire, tricking me into spinning around in circles. Sáo had mentioned that the shiny thing had a vast wealth of knowledge.

I wanted to see if it could tell me why I was here. I examined the shiny thing, Sáo had been fooling around with it earlier and had left it on. There were a variety of symbols scattered across it.

A slowly spinning triangular symbol a little ways above the center, nine different colored circles scattered across the shiny thing, a thin line leading from a dark blue circle near the bottom of the shiny thing to a blue and green one near the top, and runes so many runes. I tilted my head trying to figure out what it was. It almost looks like those maps the elder would draw in the sand.

I closed my eyes and tried to remember what he said. I tapped the triangle with a claw, if I'm right this is where I am. I traced the line to the blue and green circle, and this is where I'm going.

"No!" I whipped around. I could have sworn Sáo was asleep! I thought as I drifted over to her.

"Noo come back.. please you're so pretty," she

mumbled.

Oh not awake just sleep talking. I turned back to the map and tapped the rune above the dark blue circle, and it brightened. Neptune.

"What..?" I tapped more runes. Jupiter, Venus, Saturn. These are all names of planets.

Am I not on Neptune anymore?

No you're not.

Mother! You're back!

Yes, now listen carefully. You're being sent to a different planet, one called Earth.

Why?

Hush! I don't have long, by the time you get to Earth I won't be able to talk to you anymore.

You won't? I asked.

I'm not all powerful, I do have my limits. It's already taking a great amount of concentration and energy to talk to you right now. When you arrive you must be very careful, Earth is inhabited by other intelligent species. The Elves probably won't be bothered by you but the — dangerous — do not approach — fire —

Mother? I didn't hear what you said. Mother?

Silence.

Mother?

I floated in place for a moment, trying not to scream. I shook my fists at the roof of the cave several times before heading back to the sleeping hole. I guess I'm on my own now.

"I got it, I got it!" Sáo shouted as she zoomed after a kraken. She had insisted on me showing her how I caught kraken so easily. I watched her, mildly amused from my sleeping hole as she chased it.

She seemed weirdly attached to me for some reason, probably a city-born thing, the elder did mention that city-born would often share territories with each other.

"Be careful, swimming too fast in this small a space, you might-"

Thud. "Owwww."

I snickered softly as Sáo clutched her head.

She glared at me, "Not funny!"

"Very funny, and it's really not that hard," I said.

"Well if it's so easy why don't you do it?"

"Alright," I replied.

I shot up out of my sleeping hole, but didn't chase the kraken. Instead, I let it zoom around the room.

"So, how are you supposed to catch the kraken without chasing it?" Sáo asked, her voice tinged with sarcasm. I ignored her and watched the kraken. I waited until it started to slow down then I zipped past and around the kraken, placing myself in its path. It tried to dart away, but too late. I snatched it up with both hands.

"There, easy," I said, offering it to Sáo.

"Show off..." She took the kraken from me and examined it. "Hey, this one looks different from the others."

"I guess."

"Ya know what?" Sáo said, holding the very still kraken in her hand.

"What?" I asked slithering back to the sleeping hole.

"I think I'm gonna keep this little guy as a pet!"

I stopped in place and stared at her in confusion. "Why? It's food, you don't keep food as a pet."

"Well, he's pretty small so I don't see any point in eating him."

I hesitated, "So..?"

"I could raise him for a few months just until he's big enough to eat. Some Síren do that in the city, they catch little kraken then raise them until they're big," Sáo gently petted the tiny kraken with one finger.

I blinked slowly at her, and rubbed my gills. "I have no idea what you're saying, if you want to keep it, then keep it."

"Yay!" she said, doing a little twirl in the water. "I'm gonna call you... Squishy."

I munched quietly on a kraken as I watched Sáo and her pet kraken -Squishy-, it had only been a day since she decided to keep him as a pet, and somehow it was working. In less than a day Sáo managed to train him to respond to two basic commands.

I looked at my egg, snuggled in its nest. I don't know what you're going to be when you hatch, but I have to make sure I'm prepared to train you.

Then I noticed something, was the egg shaking? Suddenly the room began to shake. I glanced over at Sáo who gave me an equally confused look. Then out of the corner of my eye I spotted the shiny thing light up.

"Look!" Sáo swam over to it just as runes began flashing across it.

"What does it say?" I asked.

Suddenly the room lurched and flipped upside down, sending both of us flying, Sáo screamed in terror as the room spun like a sea serpent in a fast current.

"What's happening?!" one of us shrieked. Then as quickly as it started it was over, leaving us both sprawled across the room.

I groaned and flipped myself right side up. "Well, that was horrible," I said.

Sáo darted over to me holding my blue egg.

"Hey, what are you doing with that?"

She passed it to me, "It's not over yet." Then I heard a loud sound, like an ice tower cracking.

The spinning started again, the next few minutes were torture. Constant spinning and being tossed around, I couldn't tell what was up and what was down anymore. Sáo screamed somewhere to my left -or was it my right?- are we falling? If we're falling, when will we land? I slammed into something hard and blacked out.

I groaned softly and opened my eyes. Ugh, my head. I slowly pushed myself off the floor.

"Hey, you ok?"

I gave Sáo a slight nod and looked around. The cave was a mess, the shiny thing had fallen from its place and was now completely shattered, the dark circle where the kraken came from was cracked down the middle, and my egg's nest was destroyed.

"Look at that," Sáo whispered, pointing at something behind me. I turned around, there was a hole in the wall. I approached it warily, the hole wasn't very big but it was large enough to squeeze through.

"I'll go first," I offered.

I pushed my egg through then wiggled through after it. The hole was tight and for a moment I got stuck, I nearly panicked worried I was going to be stuck there forever. But then I slipped out. I breathed a sigh of relief and scooped up my egg. I looked around, the hole had led into a winding tunnel. Sáo slithered through the hole, wiggling out much easier than me. She glanced around.

"Nowhere to go but forward," I murmured. We swam down the tunnel, occasionally coming across holes that lead to caves like the one we came from until finally we reached the end.

It looked as though the tunnel had been meant to connect to a cave three times as large as the one we were in, that had been split in half. We could get out!

A soft clatter reached my frill, I turned to identify it and there, a thing, another Síren? No, something else. The creature was similar to a Síren, but it had no sail instead it was covered in this thick white seaweed. It kept digging at a rock that looked to have fallen from the tunnel wall. We would have to go around it. Sáo came up behind me and gasped.

"A vampire! Be careful, they can be dangerous!" she whispered. The vampire banged on the rock a couple more times before screaming in frustration.

"I think he's stuck," I whispered back.

"Let's find out," she whispered back. "Hey! Do you need help?" Sáo called to him. The vampire turned to us and I found myself facing two rows of absurdly large teeth.

Síren. A voice said in my head.

I was startled at first thinking it was Mother, no it was not Mother, this is a male. Sáo noticed my reaction and smiled.

"Vampires communicate telepathy, they also can't breathe under water. I'll help you get unstuck but you have to promise not to bite my head off." I blinked at him, Sáo was right those teeth could easily sever a Síren's head from their shoulders.

I promise, He replied, a long tongue flickering out

33

briefly. Sáo moved over to him and started pushing against the rock,

"Cracking ice! This thing is heavy! Echo, get over here and help!" I put down the egg and hesitatingly joined her in pushing the rock. When the rock started to move the vampire pulled, and with a final heave the rock fell away and the vampire shot free. I realized what had been stuck under the rock. He had a tail, a long winding tail that swished in the water.

Thank you, I will remember this kindness. He glanced at me, *it's not seaweed by the way, it's my fur.* He turned back to Sáo. *Bountiful hunting wherever you roam!* He called and swam off. I scooped up the egg again and looked out to see where he went but couldn't spot him.

"A vampire? Weird," I said, scratching at my gills.

"Yeah I guess, you've never seen one before right? Makes sense, they live above the ice so our species never really come across each other," Sáo replied.

"Fur..." I shuddered, "sounds itchy."

I swam out of the big cave into the open water. Sáo joined me and took a deep breath, "Wow it's so different from Neptune," she murmured. I grimaced and rubbed my gills. Too warm, this water is too warm, it hurts my gills. I thought.

"Well then," I said turning to Sáo, "this is where we part ways."

"What? Why?"

I scratched at my gills, "To find our own territories."

"But friends stick together," she protested.

"Friends? Wild-born don't have friends, we had a truce. Now that we're not stuck in the same cave together, that agreement is now void.

We're free to live alone, as we please," I turned and swam away making sure not to look back.

I stared after Echo as she swam away. She was wrong, being alone in a new environment that wasn't even on the same planet we came from was only going to kill us both.

"Well then, what do you think Squishy?" Squishy merely blinked his large eyes at me. "Brilliant idea! We are free to do as we wish, and she never said anything about following her!" I exclaimed, "After that wanderling!"

I swam off in the direction Echo went. The only thing I had to fear was being unable to hunt anything and starving to death. Echo had something else to fear. Síren with open gills were always more prone to gill-rot.

✦ *Chapter 5* ✦

The first few days that I was on my own were good. I wasn't even looking for territory just getting a feel for the wildlife. But slowly my health seemed to spiral. It's probably just something in the water, I told myself, something new that I'm not used to yet.

I was wrong. At first I could catch food with ease, but now prey always managed to evade me. My open gills that gave me my amazing sense of smell were now swollen to the point I could barely breathe, plus the constant itchiness. I lay very still on a rock slab checking and rechecking all my symptoms. There was no mistaking it, I had the deadly gill infection that plagued all Síren, gill-rot.

I laughed out loud, to have survived being a youngling, being taken, sent all the way to Earth from Neptune, two planets that were millions of tail lengths apart, surviving a crash landing in the strange cave that brought me, only to die of gill-rot. For some strange reason I found that to be the funniest thing. I just laid there laughing for a moment.

"Echo?" a voice called. I blinked and stopped laughing, everything seemed kind of foggy.

"Who's there?" I rasped.

"It's me."

That's unhelpful.

"How is that unhelpful? I highly doubt you know that many Síren."

Did I say that out loud?

"Yes you did, have you lost your mind?"

I believe I have, but then again I am dying.

"No, you're not."

Hello, Sáo.

"Hello to you too, about time you recognized me."

No one else is that nauseatingly optimistic.

"Rude."

She carefully rolled me onto my side. "I need to clean out your gills, ok? This is going to hurt." She pressed something hard against the skin just above my gills.

This isn't so bad. I thought. Then she began scraping, it felt like she was scratching my gills out! No matter how much I thrashed she found a way to pin me down, even if I screamed and begged she ignored me and kept working.

Finally after what felt like hours of torture Sáo stopped, she took something long and tied it around my neck so it covered my gills.

"There, that should help with the infection." She looped her arms around my chest.

"What are you doing?"

"I have a cave nearby, I'm taking you to it so I can keep an eye on you, and don't worry I have your egg."

I'm not getting away from you, am I?

Sáo laughed, "Nope!"

✦ *A couple weeks later.* ✦

I stared at the egg intently. Just a few minutes ago I saw it twitch. It was a little boring, lying in this cave. But it was better than the cave that brought me from Neptune to here, I could even go outside and wander around, especially since I wasn't sick anymore! I rubbed at the seaweed wrap around my neck.

"Don't scratch," Sáo murmured from where she was resting. I glowered at her.

After that first horrible torture session Sáo had dragged me to a nearby cave. At first I was annoyed, but too sick to really do anything about it. After about a week I felt healthy enough to swim without crashing into stuff –most of the time at least– so Sáo began letting me leave the cave to swim around a bit. And that's when the escape attempts started.

Was I still sick at that point? Yes. But that didn't stop me. I wanted to leave Sáo and be a proper wild-born.

When Sáo dragged me back to the cave after my fifth failed attempt she threatened to weave a rope out of seaweed and tie me up so I couldn't ever leave the cave.

She also yelled at me about how stupid I was thinking I could survive for very long with my gills as inflamed as they were, but I was paying more attention to the 'tie me up with a rope' part of her rant. Knowing Sáo like I did, I believed her and the escape attempts stopped.

I turned back to the egg. In the few weeks living with Sáo I learned more about her.

I learned that she actually grew up with her mother, who taught her how to carve ice. She also had an older brother named Moonhunter. Sáo had spoken a lot about Moonhunter, she seemed to think very highly of him. Sáo often worried about Moonhunter, she said that he'd been captured along with her to be sent to Earth. She wondered where he was and if he was alright. I had the feeling that if Sáo hadn't met me, she would've probably set out to find Moonhunter as

38

soon as she escaped the cave that brought us to Earth. There was also some mention of a Síren named Lightscale, but Sáo didn't talk about him much. I sensed that Sáo had some guilt regarding Lightscale, but I didn't know why.

Crack.

The egg's hatching! I leaned forward excitedly, it shook slightly and cracked a little more then stopped. I tapped the egg curiously, it is hatching right? Tap, tap, the egg responded. I smiled and tapped back. The crack spread a little further, causing an eggshell piece to fall in.

A dark gray eye blinked at me, the egg made a squeaky noise and shuddered slightly. I tapped the egg again.

"Come on out little one," I whispered, "you can't hide in there forever."

The egg squeaked at me again and another piece of eggshell fell off, this one a bit larger. A little snout poked out of the hole briefly before retreating back. I smiled again. "Come out." More cracking, this time along the top of the egg. A couple of the pieces were pushed up and out of the way.

I started pulling a piece off and hesitated. Am I supposed to help the egg or is it supposed to hatch on its own? I shrugged, and peeled the eggshell piece away and gasped. A pair of dark gray eyes stared up at me from a dark blue and white face that sparkled slightly in the dim light.

Is this a kelpie?

"Oh wow, a hippocampus!" a voice said from behind me.

I flared my frill as I whipped around. "When did you get there?!" I demanded.

Sáo laughed at me. "Oh you should've seen your face, it was so cute! The way you were smiling!" She held her arms out, "I'm sorry for scaring the fearless wild-born," she teased, trying to pull me into a hug.

I pushed her away, "Don't like hugs," I muttered, "you were saying something about a hippocampus?"

"Hm? Oh yeah, well before you ask, no this is not a kelpie."

Did she read my mind?

"This is a hippocampus. While the two species are rather similar there are some obvious things that differentiate between the two."

Oh no.

Sáo took a deep breath, "The first is that while kelpies have four legs -both front and back- hippocampus only have two -the front pair- as well as a tail like our own."

I groaned, "No, please stop, I beg you."

"Also kelpies are rather limited in their color patterns, only coming in shades of pale blue like ice or very, very rarely pale purple. However, the hippocampus can come in a variety of blues and greens of any shade!"

She took another deep breath, "Hippocampus can come in different sizes too! Some Síren believe that if given the chance, hippocampus could replace the kelpie as the most popular pet! However due to hippocampus being so rare it is incredibly expensive to buy one in the city, and finding one in the wild is extremely difficult."

Yeah no, I'm not listening to two hours worth of this. I shivered. Never again. I looked at my hippocampus, who had finally scrambled out of its egg. I wiggled my fingers at it and it clumsily swam over to me. I pet it gently and gave it a quick once over.

She -as it was actually a she- seemed perfectly healthy. "Now what am I going to call you?" I asked the hippocampus as I ran my fingers through her mane. Just like her face, the hippocampus's body was dark blue with some white patterning. "How about…Larissa?"

She made a little shrill sound and nibbled my fingers "You're probably hungry huh?" I glanced at Sáo who hadn't moved and was now going on about what sounded like the pros and cons of owning a hippocampus vs a kelpie. "Come, Larissa! I'll find you a nice crab to munch on."

I zipped to the entrance, then paused and looked back. Larissa was clumsily following behind me. "Oh right," I swam over to her and scooped her up. "Forgot that you're a hatchling?"

I brought her to a spot where there were often crabs. I put her down and scooped up a crab, "This is food, see? You crack it open like this."

After hunting down and eating a bunch of crabs, we headed back to the cave.

"Now we will get yelled at by Sáo for leaving her behind," Larissa squeaked at me. "Yeah, we probably should have brought her some crab."

✦ *Many months later.* ✦

I peeked warily out of the water, eying the creatures as they sunbathed. Slowly I pulled myself onto a nearby rock to get a better look at them. The creatures were massive, a lot of them were either as big or bigger than me. And all of them had massive tusks. I shuddered, I didn't want to know what would happen to any unlucky Síren caught in those jaws. A flicker of movement caught my eye as Sáo briefly popped out of the water not too far from me.

"So. What are these?" I asked.

Sáo was quiet for a moment. "They're called walruses. We only need two. So be careful which ones you choose." I squinted at the walruses. The walrus herd was sitting on an outcropping, surrounded by water. I slipped back into the water and thought quietly on how to catch them.

Me and Sáo were currently out on a hunt. After many months of eating only salmon, shellfish, and tuna –as much as I loved tuna even I could only eat so much of it–. We all wanted something new, so when we'd found these walruses the first thing we had to know was if we could hunt them or not.

Sáo stared at the walruses, "Uhh, Echo?"

"Mhm?"

She started nibbling on her arm-fins, a nervous habit I'd noticed. "You have a plan, right?" I looked over at Sáo and smiled. "...What?" she asked.

I explained my plan, Sáo looked more and more terrified with each word.

"I have to what?!" I slapped a hand over her mouth and glanced over at the walruses. They hadn't seemed to notice Sáo's outburst.

"Calm down, you've got the easy part," I said.

"Says you! You've got the easy part, all you have to do is give them a little scare."

I offered her an evil grin. "Oh I'm sorry, you're completely right. You have to do this difficult job of herding a couple little walruses away from the rest of their herd. While I have this easy, relaxing, definitely not dangerous job of charging head first at the entire herd and hoping they don't bash my head in. Would you like to swap jobs?" I asked.

"Ok, ok. You've made your point, I'll stop complaining," Sáo grumbled. I swished my tail and peeked out of the water slightly.

"What are they called again?" I asked mischievously.

Sáo glared at me, "Walruses, they're walruses." I examined the walruses again, watching them before deciding.

"Those two," I said, pointing out the walruses I wanted. "See them?" Sáo looked over to where I was pointing.

"Yeah… I see them," Sáo said, sounding dejected. I patted her head in an attempt to comfort her, but she just glared at me. I pulled my hand away, "Right, well get going," I said.

"Oh Mother help me, this is how I die," Sáo murmured as she swam over to where I told her to go. I waited until I saw her in position then slipped into the water and approached carefully, can't mess this up just approach them, it'll be fine. I paused only about four tail-lengths away, before charging with a wailing scream. The walruses lifted their heads to stare at me for a second before panicking and fleeing towards Sáo.

I reached the shore and began clambering up, swatting and shrieking to encourage any stragglers. I looked around at all the panicking walruses in the water. Where is she? Ah, there.

Sáo had managed to separate the two walruses I wanted from the herd, and was chasing them out into the open ocean.

She's gonna need my help killing them. I slithered into the water and darted over to help. It was a bit difficult as there were panicking walruses everywhere and they kept slamming into me as they tried to get away from Sáo. After spending far too long shoving past walruses, I reached Sáo. I gave her a quick nod and darted past, shooting after one of the walrus she'd herded. The walrus saw me coming and swam away.

To my surprise, it was quite fast in the water. I'd assumed that a creature of that size would've been slow. But no matter how fast the walrus was, it couldn't out-swim me.

I grabbed it by the tail and pulled it towards myself.

It lashed out at me with its absurdly long teeth, I dodged and grabbed its head. It took a few seconds but I was eventually able to wrench the walrus's head to the side and sink my teeth into its throat.

The walrus tasted different from other creatures I'd eaten, not awful, just different. When the walrus stopped thrashing I let it go. It sank to the ocean floor. I looked around for Sáo. She was not far, still fighting with the other walrus, but she wasn't doing as well as I did.

Sáo's walrus had been driven into a frenzy, attacking Sáo and trying to get to the shore where the rest of the walrus herd was. Sáo was only just barely managing to keep the walrus back. I glanced at my walrus, it was definitely dead. I darted over to Sáo, ready to help.

I wrapped my tail around the walrus's chest, squeezing it. The walrus didn't like that and started thrashing. Not wanting to drag the fight out, I punched the walrus twice in the back of the head.

The walrus spasmed once before going still. I unwrapped my tail from the walrus and it began sinking. Sáo had backed away once she realized I came to help and was now quietly drifting nearby, watching.

"You good?" I asked. Sáo nodded, staring at the now dead walrus.

"You just… killed it with like…two punches," she muttered.

I grinned, "Practice, and also luck. Now come on, let's get these back to the cave." I grabbed the sinking walrus and passed it to Sáo before swimming down and scooping up the other one. We began the long swim back home.

"So what are these again?" I asked, several minutes later.

"For the hundredth time they're walruses, now stop

asking," Sáo replied.

It had been quite a few months since Larissa hatched. For some reason even though I wasn't sick anymore, I still stuck around. Sáo said it was because we're friends, and for some reason I believed her.

It felt nice. Living with another Síren, maybe wild-born didn't usually have friends. But that was on Neptune, the rules were different on Earth. The fact that Sáo was a much better healer than I am was a bonus though.

"Let's stop here for a break," Sáo suggested. I yawned, walruses were heavy and we still had quite a way to go.

"Hey Echo," Sáo said.

"What is it?"

"Over there," she pointed, "what is that?" I squinted at where she was pointing.

Something large that floated on the water was rapidly approaching us. Within seconds it got to us and started circling. Then a shrill pulsing noise filled the water. Sáo and I shrieked in pain, and darted, dragging our kills with us. But the floating thing kept pace, and with it, the noise.

"Drop the walruses!" Sáo called. "We can come back for them later!" I nodded and dropped my kill. Without the walruses slowing us down, we could speed up and put distance between us and the floating thing.

But still the floating thing followed us, making that horrible pulsing noise.

"Echo! Look!" Sáo pointed ahead of us. There was another one rapidly approaching from the front. I glanced around, trying to find a way out. There! A shallow cove, it will suck for us with the shallow water but the floating things would be too big to fit through the gap.

"Follow me!" I shouted and darted for the cove

entrance. Sáo followed me closely. We dove through the narrow entrance, my scales scraped against the rock.

I shrieked in terror as suddenly I was tangled in some invisible seaweed. I called out a warning to Sáo but I was too late and she crashed into me, getting herself tangled too. I thrashed and squirmed, trying to get free. Out of the corner of my eye I could see a strange tube-like thing drawing nearer to us.

Is it gonna help us? It stopped a little ways away and watched us struggle. It waited until both of the floating things caught up. Then something weird happened. A little creature fell from one of the floating things. The creature awkwardly swam over to us. It wasn't until it was right next to us that I realized it was holding something long and thin, kind of like seaweed but really stiff. The creature kept jabbering in a high pitched voice that I couldn't understand,

"What is that thing, Echo?" Sáo asked nervously.

I stared at it, "I'm not sure."

The creature moved over to Sáo and pressed the end of the long-thin thing against her neck.

"Echo? What's it-" There was a crackling noise and Sáo went limp.

"Sáo?" The creature took the end of the long-thin thing off Sáo's neck and placed it against mine. I growled at it. The creature didn't react. A sharp pain spread from my neck to my head.

When I woke up, everything was dark. I reached a hand out, it hit something. I pressed my hand against the something it was cool to the touch and hard, a wall. I reached out my other hand, another wall my tail lashed, slamming into another wall. Walls, walls. I slammed my fist into a wall repeatedly, they're everywhere. I couldn't breathe. Let me out, let me out, let me out!

"Echo!" Something grabbed my arm, stopping my punches. "Echo, Echo. look at me."

I gasped softly.

"Look at me, Echo," Sáo said.

"I can't see you," I managed to rasp. A short silence, probably Sáo rolling her eyes.

"Then look at where my voice is coming from," she replied. She grabbed my other arm, and pulled me close in a hug.

"I don't like hugs," I whispered, my eyes darting around trying to see in the solid darkness.

"I know," Sáo murmured.

I gasped and panted softly. It felt like the walls were going to crush me.

"Echo? I'm going to knock you out now."

I blinked. What?

"Echo, Echo, Get up. We've been snatched again."

"Ugh, why does that keep happening?" Realizing I was coiled up, I attempted to stretch, but only ended up smacking Sáo in the face with my tail. "Sáo? You alright?"

She nodded, rubbing her nose, "Yeah."

I pushed myself off the ground. "Where did we end up this time?"

"You've been taken by humans."

"Who said that?"

"I did."

I turned around to face the speaker. The first thing

I noticed about it was its pure white scales. Wait, Sáo? No, not Sáo, she's right behind me. Another Síren? No, it looks too wrong. In fact the longer I stared, the more convinced I became that the speaker wasn't actually a Síren.

"What are you?" I demanded.

The not-Síren chuckled, "I am a mermaid."

"Right…" I looked around. Sáo and I were stuck in a tiny container with clear walls. Very tiny, we could barely fit. Even though we were both coiled up to make room for one another, it felt cramped. The low top also meant I could accidentally knock myself out if I wasn't careful, which would be really embarrassing. The new container was smaller than the dark one, but at least I could see.

"How are we gonna escape this one?" I murmured.

"You want to escape? Well lucky you, I already have a plan," the mermaid said, flapping her tail. Her container seemed to be the same size as ours, but she didn't have to share it with anyone.

"You do?" I asked, shoving down my jealousy for her non-shared container.

"Of course, as a mermaid I have two forms, the one you see now and one with legs that allow me to walk on land. My plan is perfect so I don't mind if you two tag along," she purred.

"Echo!" Sáo hissed.

I looked over and she motioned to come closer. "Isn't this great? She knows a way out!" I whispered.

"Actually I was gonna say we shouldn't do it."

"What?! Why not?"

"Echo, I know as a wild born you naturally don't always know certain things but come on! She's a mermaid!"

"So?"

"Síren don't get along with mermaids! Never have,

never will!" Sáo swished her tail frantically. "They're the Betrayers, Echo."

At those words memories flooded my mind, things I knew but never learned. A voice that sounded like the Great Mother screaming in grief, a mermaid holding the broken body of a youngling, fear, grief, betrayal, and a deep hatred of mermaids. I shook off the memories and emotions.

"I know, but I refuse to be trapped in another small place again," I muttered, sorting through the memories and trying to make sense of them.

Sáo sighed. "Ok, we'll do it but I still don't like this."

I turned back to the mermaid, "Take us with you."

She smiled. "Of course, and please call me Cici." Cici then changed, her tail becoming legs like that of a human. She whispered something I couldn't make out and the top of her container popped open. She neatly slithered out and opened ours, I moved to climb out then hesitated.

"What's wrong dear?" Cici asked.

"We can't breathe above water," I explained.

"Oh well in that case," She muttered something under her breath and I felt myself changing. I looked down and watched in shock at my tail split in two, turning into legs like Cici's had.

"There." She reached in and pulled us out. "Now that spell will only last until you get wet again so we have to move quickly." I nodded and glanced behind me at Sáo who also nodded.

It unfortunately took a minute just to get used to having legs, but Cici was patient and led us through where we needed to go. Finally we reached the exit.

"Hang on, look." Cici pointed at something square on the wall. "Silent alarm, if you walk in front of it, it will alert all the humans someone is trying to escape." She snuck up to it, keeping herself pinned to the same wall it was on.

Then placed a hand over it and started fiddling with it. "There, now it's deactivated, come dears," she said and waved at us to follow her.

"This is where they launch the subs."

I stared at Cici. "What?"

"The tube things that probably caught you? Those are called subs, this is one of the places where they get put into or taken out of the water."

"Huh." I glanced over at Sáo, she hadn't said much at all which was unusual for her.

"Now come here. Look, see there in the water? That's a propeller. When we dive in we must be careful not to get too close to it, otherwise we would get sucked in."

"And that would be bad?" I asked.

Cici smiled at me, "Very bad." Sáo and I carefully approached the edge, wary of the spinning propeller that was just under the surface not too far away.

"Now Echo I get the feeling you're probably the strongest and fastest of us, so you go first."

I whipped around to look at Cici, "What?"

She smiled again, "Go first and make sure the way out is clear, you're the fastest so you'd have a better chance out swimming the subs."

I nodded, it made sense. I moved as far away from the propellers as I could. "See you on the other side," I said to Sáo who gave a shy grin in response. Then I jumped.

◇ *Sáo.* ◇

I rushed over to where Echo jumped and scanned the water anxiously. There! Echo's head popped out of the water, and she waved at me. She looked normal again, I guess Cici was telling the truth when she said the spell would wear off when we got wet. I waved back and Echo dove back under. I took several steps back to get a running start.

I moved to jump but Cici stepped in front of me. "Oh no dear, you're going somewhere else," she said, glancing purposefully behind me at the propellers.

She's gonna throw me in.

"This was your plan? Trick a couple of innocent Síren you just met? For what?" I asked, trying to stall for time. Time for what, I wasn't sure.

Echo will realize something's wrong if I don't join her soon right?

Cici laughed, "No particular reason, but I had the feeling you wouldn't be so agreeable if you knew I was planning to kill you."

She stepped closer to me menacingly, herding me. I glanced around nervously, Cici had me cornered near the propellers.

I glanced at her and considered my chances of outrunning her.

"Oh no you don't." Cici sang something strange and suddenly my legs reverted back to a tail. I yelped as I nearly toppled off the edge.

I looked behind me, if I'd fallen I would've been sucked into the propellers. If her plan was to push me off, it'll be harder now but I can't go forever without breathing. I need to get her talking.

"You seem to have really thought this through in the few minutes you got."

Please work, please work.

"Well I'm gonna kill you in a moment anyway," she murmured almost to herself. She clapped her hands.

"So that soundless alarm I deactivated? It's actually

51

set to go off in about a minute or so, at which point I will have tossed you in. Then while the humans are scrambling to figure out what happened, I will slip away unnoticed."

The ice slabs I used to read back home were right, merpeople really do like to hear themselves talk. "Won't they eventually realize you're gone?"

Cici shrugged, "By the time they notice -if they ever do- I'll be long gone."

I need to make her angry.

"Are all merpeople as manipulative as you?"

She scoffed, "We aren't manipulative, we just bend the truth a little. Of course you're descended from the Mother so naturally you're inferior. Children of the Great Father have the superior heritage."

In response I said something about her heritage that was so vile if my mother had heard me, she would have cuffed me in the head.

"How dare you!" Cici screamed.

It only took a second, Cici lunged at me enraged. I tensed up, everything seemed to move in slow motion. Closing my eyes I flipped onto my back and smacked her with my tail, there was a shriek of anger and a loud splash.

I opened my eyes and peeked over the edge, there was Cici. Floating in the water yelling words that even I wouldn't dare to say. I looked behind her and felt my frill and sail stiffen in fear, Cici had fallen near the propellers. I looked away.

There was a yell of shock which turned into a scream of terror, then cut off abruptly. I gagged and looked over at the propellers, they were making a weird grinding sound. I tilted my head, then suddenly they stopped spinning, instead they twitched. What's happening? Something appeared in the water, not far from the propellers. What is that? I froze in horror when I recognized her. It was Echo, she was staring at the propellers.

"No!"

BOOM!

✦ *Echo.* ✦

I waited impatiently for Sáo to come out. She's taking forever. I had already scouted around to make sure no humans would catch us. I sighed. Maybe she needs my help. I started swimming back towards where I had jumped, and nearly collided with a 'sub'.

That was close. I thought as I quickly dipped under and around it. I entered the bay where we were supposed to jump. Weird, I thought Cici said the propellers never stop. I approached them warily, then I noticed why it had stopped. The bloody remains of something -or someone- with white scales was caught between the blades. The propellers made a soft grinding noise. I blinked. Oh no.

BOOM.

The propellers exploded, sending me flying and pelting me with propeller pieces. But I didn't care, Sáo was dead.

✦ *Chapter 6* ✦

✦ *Echo.* ✦

I lay coiled up in my container, a human walked by, I huffed at it. It hadn't taken them long to re-catch me. The explosion from the propellers sent out a shockwave which had not only sent me flying, but stunned me as well making me easy prey. Can't a wanderling get a break? A couple humans stopped outside my container. I recognized one of them, it would sometimes bring me food, the other one was new to me.

I blinked at the new human, this one somehow looked more clean than the other. Like it had been polishing its scales with hard-ice. Hang on…Do humans even have scales? I leaned closer to the container wall trying to see. To my mild amusement, the shiny human mimicked me, then chattered to the other one softly.

The other human nodded and quickly walked away. I watched it curiously. The shiny human stayed, looking bored. Is it waiting for something? Suddenly a bunch of humans appeared out of nowhere and swarmed my container. I looked around, confused, what are they doing? I noticed some of the humans were carrying some strange objects but I couldn't get a good look at what they were carrying. A couple of humans crouched down, it looked like they were doing something with the bottom of my container, suddenly I noticed that the water seemed to be disappearing. Are they draining the water? Somehow the humans removed most of the water in the container, leaving me with barely enough to float in. Not even enough to float in, even with my sail lowered it was still breaching the surface.

Just then the container jerked and began sliding. The humans pushed my container to a different room. I moved around trying to comprehend where I was and what was happening but I couldn't see over the humans. Propping myself up above the water didn't help, so I submerged myself again. A couple of humans placed down some of the things they were carrying. Even though the water was muffling their voices, their chattering to one another was very loud. I coiled up trying to block out the noise.

Suddenly something poked my frill, I looked up with a snarl then shrank back in confusion. Three of the humans had somehow grown taller and were now towering over me. I hissed and raised my sail, trying to make myself look more threatening. They didn't react. Pressing myself against the wall, trying to back away from them, I spotted something. Wait a second. They're not actually bigger, they're just standing on those things they carried in.

Something that resembled a sea serpent's web dropped down and the humans began trying to wrap it around me. I watched as they reached in with their spindly, scaleless arms and grabbed at the web, looping it around me. I pinned myself to the floor of the container, trying to pull away. Of course the humans just kept wrapping it around me. I was tempted to fight back but by the time the thought crossed my mind, they had succeeded. I chuffed, given the size of the container and water level, I didn't have a chance. Suddenly I found myself being lifted out of the water. I squealed and thrashed but it was too late. The humans watched as I was raised up and out of the small container and were now scampering around beneath me. I could tell that somehow I was being held up in the air by the web the humans wrapped me in, but I couldn't see how and I didn't want to move for risk of falling to the ground. Being two tail-lengths above ground, I discovered, was a lot scarier out of the water, than it was in the water. All I could see was what was happening below me. A faint breeze brushed against my gills, I grimaced and tried to close my gills to keep them from drying out. They would only partially close. Oh right, I can't close my gills, curse you stupid genetics. At that moment I realized I was being lowered. While I was distracted the humans had brought out a different container, one that looked rather familiar. Oh no, I began to struggle, although I was afraid to fall, I'd prefer that to what would happen next. Alas, it was too late, the humans grabbed me and forced me into the container, closing the lid and plunging me back into darkness.

This was the same container the humans used to move me and Sáo before. I pressed my hands against the walls and thumped my tail.

Ok ok, this is fine. I'm fine, this is fine. Not panicking. I coiled up, closing my eyes. I'm fine.

"Hey Echo, wake up."

I blinked and shook myself.

Sáo patted my face, "Wake up," she said, I glowered at her and smacked her hand away.

"What?" I asked.

She laughed and darted off to the entrance of the cave, "Come here!"

I sighed. Sáo could be so unpredictable sometimes. I followed her over to the entrance. Sáo pointed out at the open water, "Look."

I gasped softly. They're beautiful.

Sáo grinned at me. "I thought you'd like them."

I watched the creatures as they gracefully swam past. "What are they?"

"Whales. Listen. Hear that? They're singing."

I closed my eyes and listened to the whale song. It was deep and long, it was a song of their journey. Sad, yet happy. Mourning those who were no more, but excited for those who were yet to come. It was many things at once.

I blinked awake, half expecting to see Sáo grinning at me. Instead I saw nothing but blackness, I was still inside that container the humans shoved me in. For a moment I felt a little sad. I had liked having Sáo around. I shuddered, What is wrong with me? I should be happy I'm on my own again. I wonder if Larissa's alright, the humans might not have caught her or Squishy since we left them back at the cave.

The top of the container was lifted away revealing the moon and sky. I squinted at the sudden brightness. A couple humans peeked in to look at me, and chattered to each other. Oh good, they might get me out of here. A thing that looked a bit like a sea serpent's web dropped down and the humans started trying to put it on me. I watched as they reached in with their spindly, scaleless arms and grabbed at the web and looped it around me.

Stop fooling around! Get me out!

I twisted my head to watch as they wrapped the web around my tail.

Out! Out! out!

I wiggled slightly, causing the web to tangle. Suddenly the web tightened, drawing close against my throat. I choked and grasped at my neck. The humans shrieked in terror as I thrashed in my container. I clawed at the web that wrapped around my throat. But the more I thrashed and clawed the more tangled I became.

My thrashing started to cause the container to tilt. I cried out as it tipped over, spilling water and sending me sliding. I gasped as air rushed against my gills. One of the humans rushed over to me and started pulling at the web around my neck, it called out to the other humans and some of them ran over to help. It took a minute but they managed to untangle the web from around my throat, and shoved me into a pool of water.

Finally out!

Once I could breathe properly again, I began pulling the rest of the web off myself. The humans watched me curiously as I untangled myself and tossed the web aside. One of them grabbed the web and pulled it out of the pool. Now that I was in the pool the humans seemed disinterested in me now, and slowly one by one they all left.

The pool of water they shoved me in was a weird irregular shape, about five tail lengths at its longest and about three tail lengths at its widest. It was also very shallow, barely two tail lengths deep. I wandered around the pool, there was almost an entire wall that I could see through. I peered through curiously. I could see a horizontal tunnel through the clear-wall, there was another clear-wall on the other side of the tunnel showing a different pool that looked identical to my own. If you're swimming through the tunnel you'd be able to see in both this pool and that one over there. I thought. I couldn't see anything in the other pool so

I resumed wandering.

The pool didn't have anything in it, not even a woven bed to sleep on. I sighed. Wonderful, this is even worse than the cave that brought me here.

I clutched my hands to my eyes, it was too bright. I had just been trying to sleep after a long day of being chattered at by humans, and nearly choking to death. I was about to go to sleep when suddenly the sky burst into light, the clouds glowed pink and an orb of light slowly rose above the horizon. I'd made the mistake of looking at the orb and now my eyes were stinging in pain, and the light was only getting brighter.

Even with my eyes closed and my hands covering my face I could see the light. I tentatively peaked out between my fingers and finger-webbing, searching for a place to hide. The light instantly started hurting my eyes, I squinted which didn't really help. The far end of the pool was still cast in shadow but other than that there was nowhere to hide. I darted over to the shadowy area, still covering my eyes. I curled up in a tight coil and tried not to cry.

"What is it?" I asked.

"It's the sun!" came Sáo's reply.

I blinked up at the shimmering surface of the water. I snorted, "Yeah right, the sun is a little star that's only a bit brighter than the other ones and can only be seen on very clear days."

Sáo nodded, "That's true, but only on Neptune. You

see Earth is much closer to the sun than Neptune is. Since the Earth is closer, the sun looks much bigger and brighter here. I will warn you though, our eyes can't handle that much light. So don't try to look at the sun."

"What would happen if I did?"

"Well it could actually cause permanent damage to your eyes, you see our eyes are very large, it helps us see really well in the dark."

I traced one of my eyes, "It doesn't feel very large."

"Well… hang on, I never really paid attention in biology."

Sáo was quiet for a moment. "Our eye orbs! Yes, while the size of our eyes don't seem very large on our faces, our eye orbs are massive."

"Eye orbs..?"

She pointed at her eyes, "Look! See? Eye orbs! I don't remember what they're supposed to be called."

I squinted at her, I had never considered if the different parts of an eye had specific names, it sounded like a city-born thing. Eye orbs seem like a pretty straight forward name. It then occurred to me that Sáo's eye orbs were a very pretty shade of pale green.

"So what about the eye orbs?"

"Oh right! Our eye orbs are really big to help us see in the dark underwater of Neptune. If we look at something super bright our eye orbs shrink to block out some of the light, like, how if you go into a really dark area you have to blink a few times to adjust to the darkness but in reverse. The problem is that if we look at something super bright like the sun then our eye orbs have to shrink a lot, and they're not meant to shrink that much so they can actually get stuck being small. Another thing is that it can be hard to see properly when your eye orbs are small. So if your eye orbs are stuck small due to light damage and you can't see very well then you're basically screwed!"

I jolted awake. Wonderful. Couldn't have remembered that sooner? I grumbled softly, I must have tensed all my muscles up at some point while I was sleeping because now I was all sore. I glanced up at the sky while I stretched. Can't see the sun but the sky's still pretty bright, it must be near sundown. I flopped down on the bottom of my pool. Might as well sleep until nightfall.

I dozed lightly, the floor of my pool was hard and uncomfortable, making it hard to sleep well.

"Who is there?" A low voice asked. I blinked awake and pushed myself off the floor. I looked around. "Who is there?" The voice asked again.

It's coming from the clear-wall. I approached it curiously.

I could see a creature in the opposite clear-wall. It was big, much bigger than me. It almost looked like one of the singing whales but smaller, and black and white instead of blueish gray.

"Who are you?" I didn't know the whales could speak.

"I am Echo. Who are you?" I replied.

The creature swam in a circle in front of the clear-wall. "I am called Tulva. What are you?"

I tilted my head. "Síren, I am a Síren."

The creature clicked at me, "Well then Síren-Echo, welcome to the rest of your life."

$\diamond$ *Sáo.* $\diamond$

I floated limply in my container, it had been a couple days since the explosion and I still felt terrible. If mum saw this she'd be so disappointed, I could practically hear her lecturing me.

'I spend six years teaching you all my wisdom, and the first thing you do after leaving my side is trust a slimelicking mermaid! Did you listen to a single thing I taught you in your lessons?! Merpeople are the great betrayers!' Imaginary mum yelled in my head.

I shuddered, suddenly grateful that mum wasn't here to see this.

Tap tap. I blinked and shook myself. There was a human outside my container watching me.

The human examined me, it looked kind of old. It chattered quietly to another human passing by. The new human looked over at me and nodded to the old human.

Oh tentacles, I got a bad feeling about this.

I blinked in confusion and spun around in a circle. The humans had moved me from my tiny container into a dark container. I don't know what they did with the container while I was in it, but I could feel it vibrating and sliding around.

After a rather long bumpy ride, they took me out of the dark container and dumped me into this massive one. I drifted down to the bottom, which was covered in sand. The new tank I was in was positioned up against the wall of a very large room.

I peered through the tank wall, humans really like their decorations. I could see at least four human sitting spots and a big sitting spot almost large enough for me. I shook my head, even the shop didn't have this many sitting spots, only three in the main den. The human room also had a large shelf and a table.

I explored my new tank, it really was quite big. It had some stiff plants that reached straight out of the water. I was tempted to nibble one but decided that might be a bad idea. There were also some shiny rocks and shells scattered everywhere. I picked a shell up and examined it, out of the corner of my eye I could see the old human watching me. The human watched me for a while before getting up and leaving the room. I dug a shallow hole and curled up in it to rest. I hope Squishy's doing alright.

✦ *Chapter 7* ✦

✦ *Several days earlier* ✦

Sáo clapped her hands, "ok, me and grumpy-fins over there–"
"Hey!"
"–are going on a hunting trip." Larissa swished her tail excitedly and Sáo smiled at her.
"No, you're not coming with us. We're going on our own. We're gonna be hunting walruses so we might be gone for a few days." Larissa's tail stopped swishing. "Now stay here near the cave, ok? We'll be back soon." Sáo pet Larissa's head and patted one of Squishy's tentacles. Larissa glanced over at Echo who nodded.
"Stay Larissa," she ordered. Then they both left.

-+-

Larissa stared anxiously at the cave entrance from her bed. She hated being left behind on hunting trips, if Larissa were any other type of creature she would've shot after them by now. But Larissa was a hippocampus and hippocampus obey any and all orders their master gives them.
<Larissa, calm down. I can practically see your anxiety spirling,> Squishy said.

Larissa snorted, <I'm not anxious, just worried.>

<That's the same thing.>

She shot him a glare —which he ignored— and curled up to take a nap.

A few hours later Larissa awoke to a sharp pain in her neck. She jumped out of her bed and started spinning around, she had the strangest feeling that she was in danger and should flee.

<You look distressed,> Squishy commented. Larissa glanced at him, he was sitting in his usual corner munching on something.

<I am distressed.>

<Well then, tell me: why are you distressed? No wait let me guess. You've got one of your 'feelings' again don't you?>

<How'd you tell?> Larissa asked curiously.

<Because this happens every time Echo goes somewhere without you, and every time it's nothing but your anxiety.>

Larissa chuffed in annoyance, he was right though most of the time it was nothing but her anxiety. But this time felt different.

Larissa swam in circles. <They should have been back by now.>

Squishy flicked one of his arms. <Calm down, they've been gone for barely two days.>

Larissa tossed her head. <Exactly! Two days! That's far too long! It shouldn't take two days to hunt walrus!>

Squishy closed his eyes in annoyance. <You're far too anxious. Maybe the herd moved from where we saw them last time so they had to track them down.>

Larissa tossed her mane. She could tell something was wrong. Sure most of the time she was wrong when she was worried, but she had been right the odd time.

Larissa glanced around the cave, she was trying to think. She couldn't disobey an order from Echo, but she could temporarily ignore it if she was given a new order. Larissa stared at the cave entrance. What was she supposed to do? Echo told her to stay at the cave. Sure Larissa knew that she was often a bit anxious and that it tended to flare up when Echo wasn't around, but she was positive something was off.

Larissa glanced over at Squishy who was cracking mussel shells, if she went to go find Echo she couldn't go on her own. Squishy had to go with her. He was very smart and could help her find Echo much quicker. Of course Squishy was rather lazy and most likely wouldn't want to leave the cave, but even if he didn't come she could get him to give her an order that would free her to look for Echo.

<Larissa.>

<Yes?> She asked, trying to seem innocent.

<I order you to stay inside for the rest of the night and relax for once.>

Larissa winced. Relaxing was not something she did, at least not when Echo wasn't around.

Well, he said to stay inside for the rest of tonight so I just have to wait till tomorrow.

--✝--

Larissa stared out the cave entrance. <What if they're in trouble?>

Squishy rolled his eyes. <I highly doubt there's anything in the ocean Sáo and Echo can't handle.>

Larissa glanced at him, he was sitting in the corner stacking rocks. <But what if they come across something

new that they can't?>

Squishy ignored her and continued stacking rocks.

She nibbled a hoof. <Can't you just help me look a little? Just to look around a bit?>

<No, Sáo said to stay near the cave.>

Larissa rolled onto her back and waved her legs. She sighed loudly.

Larissa glanced over at Squishy who was ignoring her. She sighed louder, and beat her tail against the floor for good measure. Three of Squishy's tentacles rippled and twitched in annoyance. Larissa rolled onto her side and watched him. Squishy lasted five minutes of being stared at before he cracked.

<If you want to go then go,> Squishy said. Well that wasn't an order, but I can take it as one.

<Why can't you come with me?> Squishy's rockstack collapsed partly and one of his eyes twitched in annoyance.

<I have better things to do than follow you on one of your runs.>

<Like stacking rocks?>

<Yes!> Squishy snapped.

There goes that option.

<If you're not gonna help me then I'll go on my own,> Larissa huffed and darted out of the cave.

Squishy looked up from his rock stack and stared. A voice spoke in his head: "Remember Squishy, Larissa is much younger than you. You gotta look after her when me and Echo aren't around okay?"

He sighed and tossed his rock aside. As much as Larissa annoyed him, he had been told to watch her.

Squishy darted across the seafloor.

Where is she? Squishy looped around a boulder covered in mussels. Swimming so close to the seafloor meant he had to go slower, he darted over a rock.

She couldn't have gotten far.

-+-

Larissa sniffed the currents, she would have thought that Echo would have left some scent for her to track. But she was wrong, she couldn't smell anything. Larissa sighed. Maybe it was just my anxiety.

<There you are.> Larissa turned to see the speaker and promptly found herself wrapped up in tentacles.

<Squishy! You came!> She cried.

<Yup, came to drag you back to the cave,> he responded, and started swimming back the way he came dragging her with him. <Can't have you wandering off and getting yourself hurt, Echo would kill me.>

Larissa wiggled slightly but Squishy held her tight.

<Nope, not happening.>

Larissa squealed in frustration.

Suddenly she stopped and sniffed the water. <Do you smell that?>

Squishy adjusted his grip. <If that's supposed to trick me into stopping so you can escape, you're gonna be very disappointed.>

Larissa craned her neck trying to find the scent again. <No, I'm serious. I really smell something.> Squishy sighed and stopped, Larissa could hear his beak clacking softly. <Do you smell it?> She asked.

Squishy was quiet for a moment, <yes, what is it?>

Larissa's nose twitched. <Blood.>

Squishy blinked, his curiosity and predatory instincts piqued.

Squishy released Larissa from his tentacles. <Your

sense of smell is much better than mine, can you track it?>

Larissa pricked her ears forward, <easily.>

The pair wandered for a while, Larissa in the front following the scent, Squishy in the back following Larissa with a tentacle wrapped firmly around her tail to keep her from darting off.

After a few minutes Larissa stopped. <Here!>

<I don't see anything,> Squishy said.

Larissa dove down to the sea floor, <the smell's coming from down here!> she called.

They searched around the area a bit before finding two abandoned carcasses.

Squishy prodded the carcasses with a tentacle, <yup that's a walrus.> He turned one over and examined it. <Looks like the scavengers have gotten to them, but this is definitely the work of Echo and Sáo.>

Squishy picked up a walrus with two of his tentacles and took a bite. Larissa sniffed the other carcass, it looked completely untouched by Síren. She gave the area a quick scan.

No one nearby, why would they leave these perfectly good walruses? Two are plenty for the four of us to eat. She glanced over at Squishy who was already eating the other walrus. Larissa gave him a nudge with her snout.

<Mm, what?>

<Come on, we haven't found Echo and Sáo yet! Finding these means we gotta keep looking!>

Squishy blinked at her. <How do you know this isn't just a stash and they're getting more food?>

Larissa poked him again. <I know kraken can eat a lot, but I doubt even you can finish a whole walrus on your own.>

Squishy sighed and wrapped two more tentacles

around his walrus. <Alright let's keep looking.>

Larissa gave the carcases a good sniff. One of them had the faint scent of Echo. A faint scent was still a scent. Larissa darted off following her nose.

-+-

They continued on for a couple hours, trying to follow the faint scent. Eventually the scent flickered out so they stopped for a break near a small cove. Squishy started eating the walrus he had brought.

Larissa stared out at the wide open ocean. Where did they go? She wondered. Larissa closed her eyes and began to think. There wasn't anything wrong with the walruses so why did Echo and Sáo leave them? Why does the scent wander around with no pattern? Why did Echo and Sáo disappear?

Larissa turned to Squishy and asked him her questions. He stopped eating for a moment to think.

<Well, thinking back on where we found the carcasses, they weren't exactly hidden were they?>

Larissa tried to remember. <No, they looked like they were just dropped there.>

Squishy did a little nod. <Right, so I think that Sáo and Echo did drop them. Maybe they were being chased by something and needed to lose the extra weight.>

Larissa considered what he said. <Why didn't you say something earlier?>

Squishy gave the kraken equivalent of a shrug. <You didn't ask.>

Larissa resisted the urge to bite him, Squishy was smart. Smarter than her. But he wasn't very forthcoming with information, often keeping stuff to himself unless asked.

Larissa sniffed the water again. <I got the scent

again!> she cried. Larissa darted to the cove. <The scent's coming from here!> she called as she wiggled inside. It was a bit tight, but Larissa fit through.

Squishy approached the entrance warily, he reached a couple tentacles in and felt around before pulling his tentacles out again.

<What are you doing?>

<Can't fit through the gap,> he replied.

Larissa rolled her eyes and started looking around for the source of the smell. There! The smell was coming from a piece of web that was caught on a rock.

Larissa sniffed the strange piece of web, it had the faint scent of Echo on it. It also smelled like something else. She leaned closer to examine it. The web looked like it had been torn off of a larger piece of web. She glanced over at Squishy who was waiting in the entrance, <do you know what this is?> she asked.

He squinted at the piece of web. <I can't see it very well from here, bring it closer.> Larissa grabbed the web in her mouth and pulled it off the rock. She wiggled out of the cove, Squishy took the webbing from her mouth and examined it.

<I'm not sure what it is, I don't recognize it. Whatever made this probably took Sáo and Echo.> He tried stretching it in different ways. <It's like sea serpent webbing but tougher.>

He brought it near his beak and nibbled it. <Bleh, tastes terrible.>

Larissa blinked at him. <Why would you try to eat it?>

<Why not?>

Larissa sighed. Squishy was always thinking of his stomach.

<Do you smell anything else?> Squishy asked.

Larissa breathed deeply. <No… I can't smell anything else,> she murmured.

Squishy's eyes softened and he gently patted her head with a tentacle. <Hey, you tried. Let's go back to the cave. We'll be able to plan what to do next after a good day's rest and some food.>

<…ok.>

-+-

Larissa lay coiled up in her bed. They had gone back to the cave and rested, but she wasn't feeling hopeful. Larissa sighed, they were never gonna find Echo and Sáo.

<Hmmm.> She glanced at Squishy, who was still playing with the piece of web they found.

<What?>

<Well, I'm just thinking this doesn't really seem like anything from the ocean.>

Larissa repositioned herself. <So?>

Squishy gave her a 'must I explain everything' look.

<So, if it's not from any creature in the water it must be from the land-dwellers.>

Larissa's head shot up. <You think land-dwellers took them?>

Squishy flicked a tentacle. <I think it's possible.>

Larissa blinked at Squishy. <So then what do we do?>

Squishy patted her head. <We find a land-dweller.>

Larissa stared up at the rocky coast. <Are you sure we're gonna find a land-dweller here?>

Squishy shrugged a tentacle, he was staying back a bit as the water was too shallow for him. <Sure, why not?

We're looking for a land-dweller, that's land.>

Larissa glanced back at him, his reasoning didn't seem reliable but she had no better ideas. She swam a bit closer to the coast.

The duo were fortunate as at that moment a young witch-boy was wandering through the brush heading to the ocean. He was planning to practice his fire-welding skills while he was swimming so he didn't accidentally set anything on fire.

He placed his backpack on the rocky ground, quickly stripped down to a thin swim shirt and shorts, and sat down on an outcropping boulder to dip his toes in. He shivered, he hated the cold but after the last incident he was banned from practicing anywhere else.

He stared at the water's mesmerizing surface. He squinted, it was hard to tell but it almost looked like something was approaching him.

Larissa popped her head out of the water. The land-dweller watched her curiously.

"A horse?" The horse swam a little closer and he could see that while the front half looked like a horse the back half definitely did not. The witch-boy automatically ran through all the water-dwelling horses species that he knew.

"You're a hippocampus."

The hippocampus snorted as if to say 'really? I hadn't noticed' out of the corner of his eye he spotted slight movement. He peered over the hippocampus.

There was something behind it, pretty big. Maybe about the size of a small car. Can't tell what it is though.

"So then what brings you so close to the coast?" he asked. He didn't expect an answer but the hippocampus was happy to give one. It filled its mouth with water and sprayed him in the face.

"Ah," he wiped the water off and smiled at the hippocampus.

Let's do something impulsive.

The witch-boy closed his eyes and murmured a few words in an ancient language. Then blinked and smiled again at the hippocampus.

<What was that? What did you do?>

The witch-boy resisted the urge to celebrate having successfully cast the spell. "I cast a translator spell, I wanted to see if it would work on an animal." He motioned to Larissa, "We can understand each other now, so what's your name?"

Larissa twitched her ears. A spell? What's that?

<I'm called Larissa.>

The witch-boy dipped a finger into the water and shivered. "My name's Dei. So what brings a creature like you up to the surface."

Larissa dipped her head in and out of the water. <We're looking for our- for our friends.>

Dei nodded. He didn't know much about hippocampi but he did know that they were extremely loyal to their masters, this one had probably gotten separated from its master and was now looking for them.

Dei cleared his throat, "Right, so unrelated question: Is that mysterious dark shadow down there a friend of yours or should I be worried?"

Larissa glanced back at the shadow. <Oh, that's just Squishy. You're fine.>

Dei squinted at the shadow. "Interesting name for a hippocampus," he commented.

<Squishy's not a hippocampus. He's a kraken.>

Dei resisted the urge to jerk his legs out of the water. "Ah, so your friends are missing. You're here. So do you need my help?" he asked.

74

Larissa nodded, <yes, me and Squishy tried to look for them but all we found was this web thing.>

Dei blinked, web thing? "Do you have it? I might be able to tell what it is."

Larissa disappeared under the water for a minute before reappearing. <Wait a second, Squishy dropped it.>

Two minutes later a pale purple tentacle reached up, out of the water holding something thin and white. Dei took the white thing and examined it. It was slightly torn around the one edge.

"This is part of a net," Dei said.

Larissa tilted her head. <What's a net?>

"It's a thing humans use to catch stuff," he looked at Larissa. "You sure she was tangled in this?"

Larissa bobbed her head. <Positive. Her scent is on it. Why?>

Dei fiddled with the net. "Well if she touched this then I can use it to cast a seeking spell to find her."

Larissa's eyes widened. <You can use that little thing to find Echo? You can do that?>

He smiled. "Yup, seeking spells are easy, to find someone all I need is something they've recently touched, or with objects I just need something similar to the thing I'm trying to find. I use it to find my socks all the time."

Larissa floated in silence for a moment. This land-dweller can find Echo! She quickly dipped her head underwater to tell Squishy the good news.

<Do it, do you need anything to cast the spell?> she asked, after telling Squishy.

Dei shook his head, then hesitated. "No, actually I need silence, I gotta concentrate to cast the spell cause I'm not used to using this spell to find living creatures." The witch-boy closed his eyes, and started muttering under his

75

breath.

He stayed like that for several minutes. Larissa was about to say something when suddenly the net began to glow and a beam of light shot out of the net, soared over Larissa's head, and zipped down the coast into the distance. Larissa stared after it in amazement. Dei quietly chuckled, and stood up grabbing his backpack as he did.

"Well come on then!" he said cheerfully. "Let's go find your missing master!"

✦ *Chapter 8* ✦

✦ *Echo.* ✦

I stared up at the dangling fish, in confusion. Just a few minutes ago a human approached my pool with a basket and a long rod. It had taken a fish out of the basket, attached the fish to the rod, and was now using the rod to dangle the fish over my pool.

What on Neptune is it doing? I noticed Tulva appear in the clear-wall.

"Hey, Tulva. What's this human doing?" I asked. He seemed like he'd had a lot of experience dealing with humans.

I hesitantly swam to just under the hanging fish.

Is that tuna?

"What is it doing?" Tulva asked, he was unable to see what was happening.

I swam in a circle, "It's dangling a fish from a rod above my pool."

"Do not attempt to eat it." He warned.

"Why? It's just hanging there. I bet if I launch myself I'd be able to grab it," I said, already calculating how to get the tuna. I could practically taste it already.

"It is trick. Human wants you to jump out to get fish."

"Why?" I asked, hesitating.

"It is training you, if you do it once human will make you do it over and over again."

"So, just ignore the fish?" But tuna?

"Yes. Be careful, that human sees itself as your trainer. It will try to make you do many tricks, avoid doing them as much as possible." I looked up at the fish again and grumbled softly before turning away.

-✦-

I stared up at the hanging fish. It had been three nights since the human had brought out the rod. My stomach growled, no one had come to feed me since the rod had been put up. The only thing the human would do was put a new fish on the rod and get rid of the old one every evening.

Sure I could live for three nights without food, I could survive several weeks without food. But I was still hungry. I glanced back at the clear-wall, Tulva wasn't there. I looked back up at the fish, my stomach growled louder. Tuna....
I glanced around again. Tulva wouldn't know, and I was really hungry.

I got the tuna on the first try, yanking it off the rod as I leaped. On the second jump I grabbed the rod, it barely lasted a minute carrying my weight before snapping. I pulled the broken part of the rod into the pool and stabbed it into the bottom of the pool. The hard floor cracked. I grinned evilly. The humans will have lots of fun trying to get this out.

And they did. The human who usually brought my food spotted it first, it left and brought another one. Both humans stood in front of my pool staring at the broken rod with what I assumed to be confusion. After a little while a third human joined them. I drifted over to the clear-wall where Tulva was already waiting.

"You did something."

"Yeah... sorry," I said sheepishly. "But it was tuna! I had to have it." Just thinking about the tuna made my stomach growl.

"You risk what little freedom you have. For tuna," Tulva said blankly.

"What? I like tuna!" I snapped.

There was a soft rumbling sound. I looked around nervously, trying to find the sound before realizing where it came from.

Tulva was laughing at me.

He said something in a different language. A language made of clicks and whistles, and something occurred to me. I waited a bit for him to calm down, he had found my mischievous doings surprisingly amusing which I had not expected.

"Hey Tulva..."

"Yes?"

"How can you speak Sírenese?"

"I do not understand question."

"Well you're an animal –no offence– and in my experience animals don't speak Sírenese. So how come you can?"

"Ah, you are not first Síren I have met."

"I'm not?"

"No, there was another, his name was Moonhunter. He taught me how to speak your tongue."

Moonhunter...Why do I recognize that name? "Where is he?"

"I do not know, he was very difficult for humans. He refused to eat, would scream every time someone approached his pool, and kept cracking glass. Eventually the humans got rid of him, just few days before you came here. It is strange though, I thought your kind spoke with your mind."

"What?"

"The other Síren didn't speak with his mouth, when he spoke I could hear him in my head."

A telepath?

A memory appeared in my mind.

"You.. have a brother?"

"Yes! Why is that so hard to believe?!"

I shrugged. "I don't know," she has a brother. "Who is he?" I asked.

Sáo flicked her frill up and down. "His name is Moonhunter, he's my older brother. He got caught along with me."

I blinked the memory away. Ahh so that's where I know the name. Sáo would be happy to know he's survived this long. I straightened. I have to find him, for Sáo.

"Ughhhhh, does this human ever give up?!" I demanded, flopping down on the hard floor of the pool after a long night of the human doing practically everything to try to get me to do a trick. Tulva laughed at me from his pool.

"I am afraid not. Humans are very persistent."

I grumbled, "You don't have to suffer through it. I don't think I've seen you do any of the stupid things the human keeps trying to get me to do."

"No, they do not. I have forced them to give up on me."

I shot up off the ground. "Really? Tell me!"

Tulva was quiet for a while. "I killed my trainer," he said calmly.

I froze in place, processing what he said. "You..killed it?"

Tulva nodded. "Yes, at least I believe I did. I am not entirely sure I did. Other humans stopped me so I do not know."

We were quiet for a little while. Both of us next to our separate clear-walls. I was laying right next to my clear-wall. Facing away from Tulva.

"I miss it."

I jumped a little at Tulva's voice. "Miss what?"

"Open ocean, it's freedom, I miss my pod."

"Your pod?" I turned towards Tulva curiously.

"My mother, father, aunts, uncles, my sisters, brothers and cousins. I miss them." He turned back to me. "What about your pod, tell me about them."

"Well… Síren are usually more solitary creatures. But I did live with a couple others."

"Tell me."

"One was a hippocampus, I found her as an egg. Her name's Larissa, she must be so worried."

"She was not caught?"

"No.. it was a hunting trip. We left her behind."

"Others?"

"Yes, a kraken named Squishy and…"

"None of your kind?"

"There was one other Síren. Her name was Sáo. But she's dead now."

"I am sorry."

"Not your fault, it was mine."

Tulva was quiet for a moment. "There is more to tell, speak, I will listen."

I took a deep breath. "I was a fool. Normal wild-born are supposed to live alone, I learned that from the Great

Mother when I was a youngling. Sure, I didn't really like the idea but I didn't argue. Things were the way they were supposed to be. Then I got snatched and everything changed, I was alone in a small cave for a while. Then another wanderling was in the cave with me.

At first all we did was fight, but after a while we got used to each other. Slowly we became friends. At first I didn't like it, but over time I warmed up to it. But now she's dead and it's my fault, and I can't stop thinking about her.

I don't understand. Why do I feel so horrible? I feel sad, but angry too. Not just at myself either. The mermaid, the humans as well. I don't get it."

Tulva watched me quietly, waiting until I finished. "You are grieving."

"What?"

"Grieving the loss of your friend. You must find something to do with this grief."

"Moonhunter. The other Síren you knew, I need to find him, he's Sáo's brother. She wanted to find him, but didn't want to leave me behind."

Tulva nodded. "You want to tell him. I do not know where the humans took him. But I have an idea of how you can find him."

I coiled up by the clear-wall.

"You are not done."

"I just can't help but feel that this is my punishment for trying to change my nature."

Thud!

I jerked up and turned to face Tulva, the orca had slammed his head into the clear-wall.

"Do not think thoughts like that. They will poison your mind. Promise me you will not think like that again."

I blinked in shock, my frill swishing forward in the

default position. "Uhh sure."

Tulva slammed his head into the clear-wall again. "No! Promise me!"

I took a deep breath and looked Tulva in the eye, "I promise."

He backed away from the clear-wall, satisfied with my answer. "Good. tell me if you start to think like that again."

"I will, what was your idea to find Moonhunter?"

I stared up at the trainer, its back was to me. I blinked, Tulva's words echoing through my mind.
Moonhunter was a general pain to the humans but it was the last thing he did that pushed them over the edge.

I took a deep breath.

"Do it," Tulva whispered from his pool.

I glanced at him, "What about you? You'll be all alone in here again"

Tulva opened his mouth in a toothy smile, "Echo. I am old. I have lived long life. There are many things I regret. But I do not regret knowing you. You are young, you have much life left to live. Do not worry about me, I will be alright. Do it. Go back to ocean. Go back for me."

I nodded. For Tulva.

I swam down to the bottom of my pool and turned around to look up at the human. I charged, launching myself up out of the water, my mouth wide open.

The human didn't feel a thing.

✛ *The kraken, the witch, and the hippocampus.* ✛

Larissa, Squishy, and Dei quietly wandered along the coast following the glowing beam of light that would hopefully lead to Echo and Sáo. Dei walked around and over boulders and across sand as he went, Larissa following him in the shallow waters occasionally dragging herself along by her front legs when it was too shallow, and Squishy in the deeper waters.

Finally Dei stopped and squinted out at the beam, raising a hand to block the glare of the sun. The beam had veered away from the coast out into the ocean.

"Hmmm."

Larissa bobbed her head in and out of the water. <What is it?>

Dei pointed out at the beam of light. "The trail leads that way but I can't go any further."

<Why?>

"I can't swim."

<You can't swim yet when we found you, you were at the ocean, that doesn't make sense.>

Dei grinned. "Well, technically I can swim. I just can't swim very well, the cove you found me at was only about eight feet deep. So I wasn't too worried there, But here?" He shivered. "Nope."

Larissa dipped under the water to speak with Squishy.

<Well? What's the holdup?> He asked.

<He says he can't swim.>

Squishy blinked his large eyes a couple times. <You're joking.>

<Wish I was. Now what.>

Squishy looked up at the beam of light trailing out towards the open ocean. <I think that our land-dweller has served his purpose. Follow me, I'll lead.>

Larissa nodded. Squishy darted off, Larissa hesitated

a moment and glanced back at Dei who was standing on the shore. She darted off with Squishy.

Dei squinted out at them. "What are they doing?" Realization. Dei splashed into the shallow water. "Hey! Wait!" he called, but it was too late, they were gone.

-+-

Squishy and Larissa followed the beam of light for about twenty minutes before Squishy stopped. Larissa slammed into him.

<Watch it!> Squishy snapped.

<You're the one who stopped. Why did you stop?>

Squishy gestured to the beam of light. <It doesn't go any farther.> Larissa swam to the surface to look at the beam. It had stopped in midair. She dived down past Squishy to the seafloor. She scanned around the area. It was completely flat with no sign of other living creatures.

Squishy joined her. <She's not here. Neither of them are. We would have seen them.>

Larissa kicked at the ground. <Do you think he was lying when he said the spell would lead to Echo?>

<I don't think he was lying. But it's hard to say, I don't know much about magic.>

Larissa sighed. <So now what do we do?>

Squishy pointed back the way they came. <When in doubt, go back a step,> he said.

Larissa sighed. <Alright. Let's go find the land-dweller.>

Dei was surprisingly easy to find. Larissa and Squishy found him exactly where they left him, sitting in the sand.

"So. I assume you figured out why you need me right?"

<The beam of light just stopped above the ocean. It didn't lead anywhere,> Squishy said.

Dei grinned, "Yeah that's because there's a limit on how far the spell reaches. Without me the spell won't go further."

<Why didn't you say that earlier?!> Larissa demanded.

Dei shrugged, "Well I didn't think you'd leave me here."

Larissa bobbed her head in and out of the water.

"I still can't swim though."

<I can fix that.> Squishy said and reached out. He grabbed Dei with three tentacles and yanked Dei towards him.

"Waaaiiiiih!" Dei squealed.

Squishy plopped Dei on Squishy's back and started following the light out to the sea. Larissa laughed at the terrified expression on Dei's face as he clung to Squishy for dear life.

-+-

About an hour later they approached an island, the beam of light brought them around the island and pointed towards a large floating thing.

"Oh shoot! Get back!" Dei hissed. Squishy stopped moving and Larissa slammed into him. "Aieeee," Dei cried, struggling to stay on Squishy's back.

<What is it?> Larissa asked, watching the floating thing curiously.

Dei clung to Squishy, "It's a human boat and not just any boat. It belongs to The Guild," he whispered.

<What's the guild?>

86

"Not what, *who*. The Guild is a large organization of humans dedicated to hunting down and capturing all supernaturals on Earth. My older sisters work for the SPF and they tell me all sorts of horror stories about some of the supernaturals they rescue from these guys," Dei whispered.

<We have to go there, the trail leads there!> Larissa said.

"Hang on a sec, I'm thinking," Dei said. He sat down on Squishy and closed his eyes, muttering to himself.

"Larissa, I need you to get me some things."

<Like what?> She asked impatiently.

"A small stone, some seaweed or algae, and a pearl if you can find one."

<Why?> Larissa demanded.

"Just do it!"

<Do it Larissa, I'm curious what he has planned,> Squishy said.

Larissa huffed and dove under.

<What exactly do you have planned?> Squishy asked after Larissa left.

Dei ignored him.

<Hey, what are you doing?> Squishy poked Dei in the stomach.

"I didn't cast a translator spell on you, so if you're trying to talk to me I can't understand you."

Squishy poked him again.

"Please stop, I'm trying to concentrate."

Squishy was about to poke Dei again when Larissa popped out of the water. She had an algae covered rock in her mouth, she spat it out onto Squishy's head and stuck her tongue out.

<Bleh, I hope that's good enough for you cause that was nasty.> Larissa said, her tongue still hanging out.

Dei's eyes flicked open and he took the rock.

"Oh yeah this is good– ew it is nasty." He glanced at Larissa. "No pearls?"

She shook her head. <Sorry, couldn't find any. Now what do you need it for?>

Dei gripped the rock in both hands and started whispering under his breath. Larissa tilted her head. Suddenly Larissa's nose felt like it was tingling. She shook her head and attempted to paw at her snout, then froze as she realized she couldn't really see her legs. She turned and looked over herself, she was almost completely invisible.

"That burning sensation you're probably feeling is a sensory spell, it'll enhance your sense of smell long enough to find a new component."

<What's a component?> Larissa interrupted.

"It's something that's used for a spell. The piece of net you gave me was a component." Dei took a deep breath. "The second spell is a camouflage spell, you're not invisible but you're pretty close to it. The humans won't be able to spot you as long as you're careful. What you're looking for is something with Echo's scent, most likely not Echo herself. Be quick, keeping multiple spells active is tiring," Dei rasped.

Larissa nodded and darted away.

Larissa swam closer to the human structure. Dei called it a boat. A long tube left the boat and for a moment Larissa thought it was coming at her, but the camouflage spell worked as the long tube passed by. Alright, just gotta find something with Echo's scent on it. Sounds pretty simple.

Larissa took a deep breath, trying to smell Echo's scent. She wandered around the area, unsure what she was looking for. She sniffed around, the entire area was a mess. Large pieces of some strange material that almost looked like rock but not quite. Larisa swam up to a piece and tapped a hoof against it. The not-a-rock made a dull clinking sound.

Larissa swam around aimlessly. I don't know what I'm doing. She thought. Suddenly a soft scent tickled her nose. What's that? Larissa followed the scent down to the ground.

She nosed a piece of sharp, shiny material away. Larissa yelped when the sharp thing cut her nose.

There! One of Echo's scales! She carefully grabbed it in her mouth. This definitely has Echo's scent! She moved to return to the others but hesitated when something flickered in the corner of her eye.

Larissa looked down at her legs. She could see them. The spell's wearing off! She checked around for any long tube things. None around but one could come at any time, I gotta get back to the others. Larissa darted away, sticking close to the seafloor. Suddenly there was a sharp snapping sound in her ear and all the strong scents disappeared, Larissa took a second to glance at her legs. She was completely visible. What happened to the spell? She wondered.

Meanwhile several miles away Dei groaned softly and toppled over into the ocean.

Larissa took a deep breath, ok. This is fine. She glanced around worriedly. I found the thing, now all I have to do is get back to Squishy and Dei. Larissa swam out into the open water. Wait. Where's the others?

After several panic stricken minutes of wandering around and worrying she was gonna be spotted by the humans. Larissa finally found the spot by the coast where she had left the others. She swam over to Squishy. <I got it, let's go!> she called, trying not to drop the scale in her mouth.

Squishy carefully took the scale from her mouth and examined it. <Echo's?>

Larissa nodded, <yup! Now where to next?> Larissa suddenly felt something was missing. <Hey, where's Dei?> She asked, realizing that the witch-boy wasn't on Squishy's back anymore.

"Up here."

Larissa looked up, following the sound of his voice. Dei was perched on top of a large rock that reached out of the water. <What are you doing up there?> she asked.

"Trying to dry off."

<Oh. Is it working?>

Dei slid off the rock onto Squishy, "No." Squishy passed him the scale.

<Are you gonna do the spell?> Larissa asked.

Dei stared at the scale in his hand, distracted.

<Dei?>

He blinked and looked over at Larissa. "Sorry, What?"

She motioned at the scale with her snout, <are you gonna do the spell?>

Dei blinked again, the words for the spell floated through his head. Dei shook his head, he'd cast a lot of spells today. Three fast travel spells to get to the ocean before he even met Larissa and Squishy, a translator spell, a seeking spell, a sensory spell, and even a camouflage spell. He needed food to replenish all of the energy he'd used.

Food. His stomach growled softly. Dei reached instinctively for his backpack only to find it wasn't there.

<Dei? Is something wrong?>

Dei was racking through his memory, panicking, trying to remember. Did he drop it during the ride?

<Dei?>

No wait. He'd left it on the beach where Larissa and Squishy tried to ditch him. He'd taken it off because it was hurting his shoulders from carrying it for so long and hadn't had gotten a chance to pick it up again before Squishy'd grabbed him. The backpack had food that he needed.

"Head back to shore first, I can cast spells better on dry land," Dei murmured. Slight lie, since he had never cast a spell on the water before, but he really did need that food.

Larissa examined the witch-boy. He looked a bit pale and shaky. <Are you alright?> Larissa asked, concerned for her friend.

"Yeah, just tired. Not used to casting so many spells at once."

She nodded, not really sure about that but pleased that he was ok. <To the shore!> Larissa cried darting off towards the beach.

"Does she have a limitless supply of energy or something?" Dei asked.

<Nah, I'm pretty sure she just leeches all of my energy away while I sleep.> Squishy replied, swimming after Larissa. Dei laughed softly.

✦ *Chapter 9* ✦

✦ *Echo.* ✦

I shook my head, pulling at the gag over my mouth. Humans were running around my pool in a panic. After the trainer human died two other humans –who I hadn't noticed before– started screaming. Soon several more humans joined them, and shortly afterwards a dozen humans were around my pool. I'd glanced around at all the chaos and slipped back into my pool.

The next morning I woke up to three humans fishing me out of my pool with hooked rods. Before I could wake up completely the humans had pinned me down and gagged me. I growled and thrashed but I couldn't move. The three humans were keeping me pinned. One human –the shiny human– approached and chattered to the others. I could see more humans appearing, they were carrying what looked like a large container. Well, that was fast.

Many long suffocating minutes later, the humans managed to haul me into the container and shut it. I could feel them moving it, and heard one of them yelling in a high pitched voice, I coiled up. Wonderful. Stuck in a tiny dark container once again. I closed my eyes so I wouldn't be able to see how dark and smothering it was.

I did what you told me to do Tulva, I hope you're right on what happens next.

✦ *The previous day*. ✦

"Echo, are you certain you want to do this?" Tulva asked.

I chuffed in amusement. "Yes, I'm certain. This was your idea. Why are you so nervous now?"

Tulva shook his head. "I do not know, I think I am worried for you."

I offered him a small smile. "It's alright. I can handle myself. I have to do this."

Tulva stared at me for a moment. "You want to find brother of your deceased friend."

I looked up at the surface of the water. "Yeah, I know Sáo cared about him a lot. He needs to know what happened." I looked back at Tulva, "I need to tell him."

Tulva opened his mouth with a smile. "Then I will do what I can to help you. Once you attack your trainer, other humans will most likely send you away. The chances you end up in the same place as Moonhunter are slim but you never know."

"What if they put me back in the ocean?"

"I do not know if they will send you back to ocean, they did not send me back. Of course perhaps you get sent somewhere else and you learn he has already escaped. You are much more likely to be able to escape from wherever they take you than you are from here. This place is nowhere near ocean, trust me I know."

I pressed a hand to the clear-wall. "Hey Tulva? Thanks… for everything."

Tulva bumped his clear-wall with his nose. "Good luck."

-✦-

I smiled to myself, still keeping my eyes closed. Tulva... I'll miss you, don't worry I'll get back to the ocean for you.

I yawned, suddenly hit by a wave of exhaustion. Well nothing to do for now but sleep. I scratched an arm.

Hm? I cracked open an eye to examine my claws, there was a scale stuck under one. I pulled the scale out from under my claw. Weird. Still keeping my eye mostly closed, I looked at and poked the spot where the scale came off.

That's strange. I rubbed at my arm again. Why are my scales falling out? I squinted at my arm. Can't see anything in this container. I'll have to wait until they take me out of it. I stopped focussing on my arm and noticed the crushing darkness of the small space. I squeezed my eye shut,

-✦-

I woke up to the sound of humans talking. I yawned. Guess they're nearly done moving me. Suddenly the container rattled and jerked up and down. I cried out in alarm as I was sent banging into the container walls.

What's happening now?

The container dropped. I shrieked again. The top of the container rattled. I shook my head and looked up, someone was opening the container. I tensed up, ready to strike at any human who appeared. The top of the container was lifted off and a human looked in.

I blinked. That human had some serious muscles. Before I could react the muscular human dropped something large and flat on my head. I jumped slightly, startled. I felt the human grab me and haul me out of the container. As it picked me up it wrapped the flat thing around me. I hissed, and thrashed but the wrap was tight, I couldn't move. The human adjusted its grip, I wiggled my head free of the wrap, allowing me to see. The wrap the muscular human had me in basically looked like a really big, gray leaf. I snapped my teeth at the human, but it didn't react. It dragged me over to a long flat tank and dropped me in, releasing me from the leaf wrap at the same time. I growled. I was about to lunge for the already leaving human when a flicker of movement caught my eye.

I turned to look. There was another Síren in the tank with me. I blinked. Great, they better not try anything. I'm not in the mood for a fight. I blinked again.

Oh wait.

There was a row of bars separating me and the other Síren. He –male Síren– seemed disinterested in me. I checked out the tank. It was pretty shallow, not even one tail-length deep and with barely any room to turn in a circle. There were some scratches along the bottom, and a strange sideways hook-like thing on the top edge of the tank but nothing else interesting.

I examined the other Síren. He was slim, with light gray scales and a darker gray sail. He looked like he'd been in his fair share of fights. His sail was torn in several places, his scales were scuffed and covered in scratches.

Are you going to say anything or just stare?
I flinched. Who said that?
Take a guess, you brain-dead kraken.
I blinked at the other Síren. "Telepath."
Correct.
"I thought that power died out."
It did, for the most part.
"You seem surprisingly calm with me here."

Take a look at those bars, it would take ages to break through them. Besides that frill-tearing human wouldn't let me touch you. What about you, hm? I'm shocked you didn't even flinch to see me.

I shrugged. "Don't see the point anymore, stuck with another wanderling in a place I can't get out of? Did it once already."

Hm.

Maybe he's seen Moonhunter here. "Have you seen any other Síren in this place?"

Hm? No, as far as I know we're the only ones here.

I frowned. Falling stars! So he isn't here then? I did all that for nothing? Ugh!

Looking for someone?

I glared at the other Síren, "That trick is going to get old really quick. Can't you speak out loud like a normal Síren?"

Unfortunately, I cannot. I don't have a tongue. Seriously, who are you looking for and why? You can't ignore me forever. I can be VERY annoying when I want to be.

The other Síren began beating his tail against the bars. *Tell me, tell me, tell me!* He chanted.

I glowered at him. What a pain in the tail-fin, I bet he's a city-born.

Oi! Rude! But yes I am.

I sighed. "I'm looking for a wanderling called Moonhunter. I have a message for him."

The other Síren blinked at me. *Well, now I'm curious. What is the message?*

"It's not for you so quit it!" I snapped.

Hm? Oh right, I forgot to introduce myself. My name's Moonhunter, son of Frostsight and Flickertail. What's yours?

"No way, you're just saying that!"

He shrugged. Wait. I thought about his parents' names. If I remembered correctly, Sáo had used the same names when we first met, and now that I think about it he does look a bit like Sáo.

"Alright, I'll tell you." I hesitated, is this really a good idea?

Well?

"Sáo is dead." The other Síren froze, his mouth opened and closed several times but he didn't say anything. "She died a little over a week ago. A mermaid got her."

No.

"It's the truth. I saw it myself."

NO.

Moonhunter turned away from me and coiled up into a tight ball.

"I'm sorry," I whispered, and I curled up to rest.

I was just dozing off when something cold clamped tightly around my neck and I was shoved forcefully against the back wall bars on the opposite side of the cage. I choked and grabbed for the thing holding me. It was the muscular human, it was holding a rod with what felt like a piece of rope on the end. The rope was looped tightly around my neck, grating against my sail, for a moment I hoped that my sail might slice through the rope but that hope was short lived. The human used the rod to pin me to the ground. It was hard to see from my angle, but it looked like the muscular human latched the rod into the sideways hook-thing. It moved away from the tank for a moment before returning with the giant wrap. It wrapped me up the same way as the first time, took the rod out of the hook-thing, unlooped the rope from around my neck, and then hauled me out of the tank. It tossed the rod aside and started dragging me away.

I wiggled my head free enough to talk. "Hey! Moonhunter what's this human doing?" I called to the other wanderling. But Moonhunter either didn't hear me or didn't care to respond.

The human dragged me around for a while, I couldn't really see where it was taking me. Finally it brought me to a room with a large round pit in the center. The muscular human dragged me over to the pit.

Oh tentacles.

It tossed me in. I landed ungracefully, fortunately the pit had a bit of water in it so the landing wasn't too bad. I looked around my new surroundings. The pit was pretty large, maybe about three or four tail-lengths in diameter, two tail lengths deep, and full of dents and cracks. I poked a large crack, wonder what caused this.

I could hear the chatter of humans, I stretched myself, trying to see what was happening about the pit. The pit had slightly slanted walls and with all the cracks I was just able to climb high enough to poke my head above the pit's rim. On the way up, I found a little box attached to the pit wall. It was pointed down into the pit, I tapped it once curiously before continuing the climb. There were humans all around the pit, moving around, chattering to each other, waving small strips of seaweed around, one saw me peering around and started pointing at me and jabbering to the humans around it. The muscular human –who was nearby– spotted me, stalked over, and kicked me in the face sending me sliding back. I rubbed my nose, grumbling softly.

There was a splashing noise behind me. I turned around, there was another creature in the pit with me, it was wearing a heavy looking muzzle. I spotted two chains leading from the muzzle to the edge of the pit behind the creature.

My gills began stinging slightly and I remembered that my head was out of water and I was holding my breath. I dipped my head in and out of the water, wettening my gills and taking a quick breath. I stared at the creature in confusion. What is it? The creature looked a bit like a sea serpent, but greener and with a strange crown of spikes on the top of its head.

The creature was straining against the chains. It wanted to kill. A human reached down to the creature with a rod and poked the muzzle. With a loud clatter the muzzle fell off.

Huh?

Suddenly the creature lunged at me. I wriggled to the side just in time as the creature slammed into the wall behind me. It's fast for something so large. The creature whipped its head around to stare at me and I felt a strange urge to look at its eyes.

The creature gave a strange raspy scream. White liquid dripped from its fangs. The liquid caused the water to hiss and steam.

Acid? I stared at the creature's dripping fangs, and without realizing it slowly looked up at its eyes.

I gasped softly. What…?

The creature slithered a bit closer. I shuddered, mesmerized by the creature's bright green eyes. Can't look away. The creature swayed its head from side to side, and hissed at me. Then it screamed in triumph and lunged at me.

Come on, move! I closed my eyes. Yes! I rolled to the side just as the creature shot by me.

That was too close. The creature just missed me by a scale and slammed into a wall.

Well, if I can't look at its face, I'll just strangle it from behind! While the creature was still dazed, I lunged at it. I wrapped myself around the creature's neck, and started to squeeze. I cried out as the creature's spiny scales cut through my own. The creature bucked and thrashed trying to toss me off. I grabbed the creature's crown of spikes and clung to them.

If it tosses me off I'm done for. I coughed, my gills flaring. Oh right, I can't breathe air. I grimaced. I guess it's a matter of who suffocates first. I squeezed tighter, and clawed at the top of the creature's head. The creature slammed its snout into a wall before shaking its head causing its venom to spray. I grimaced in pain when several droplets landed on my tail. We stayed like that for several minutes, both of us choking to death.

Finally, with a soft rasp the creature collapsed on its side. Pinning me under it. I gasped desperately at the water, my gills eagerly took in the water and I regained my breath. Slowly I wiggled out from under the creature and looked around. The humans were all silent, then they exploded with noise. All of them were yelling. I covered my frill with a wince, what's got them so upset? Then the muscular human appeared and jumped down into the pit and grabbed me.

-◇- *Sáo* -◇-

I blinked, I was in the city again. How did I get here? I looked around, the streets were empty which was strange. Usually there were at least a few Síren wandering around.

I swam around, "Hello? Anyone?" I called. Where is everyone? I stopped and looked up at the signs hung up against the ice walls. I know where this is. I dashed down the street, able to move quicker without having to dodge around other Síren. I dipped into a connecting street and wiggled down a narrow alley, following a route I had swam a hundred times before.

I hesitated, having reached my destination. The shop. I wonder if she's here. I shook my head. What am I thinking? Of course she's here, she's always here. I paused and looked around, still no one, something wasn't right. I approached the shop. Stopping just near the door, I pricked my frill up to listen, I frowned. I knew that because of my short frill my hearing wasn't the best, but I should still be able to hear the sound of Frostsight carving.

I entered the shop. The shelves of sculptures were all there, Frostsight's desk where she did most if not all of her carving was there, all of her tools were there. Even the large shallow bowl where all ruined and unsalvageable projects were tossed was still in the same place behind the desk. But Frostsight wasn't.

That's weird, maybe she's up above the shop. I swam up to the living quarters. Empty. Why isn't she here? She's always here!

I swam around the living quarters, this is where I used to live. The nesting room, where I hatched. The main room, where we would eat and where Moonhunter and I would sleep. And Frostsight's private room. Moonhunter... I winced. I remembered the day we were both caught, and winced harder.

Clatter. I darted back to the tunnel that led down to the shop. There was someone in the shop, I hadn't heard anyone enter. I swam down the short tunnel. A figure was waiting with their back turned. Wait, I know that Síren!

"Moonhunter?" The figure turned around. I gasped softly and darted over to tackle him in a hug. "Moon!" I pressed my face against his chest and sobbed. "Moon... I'm sorry for ditching you when those bottom-feeding collectors came for us. I'm sorry for being a coward when you needed help. I'm sorry."

I hesitantly looked up at his face. He was giving me his look. The one that said he didn't know what I was babbling on about but was concerned for me anyway, he patted my head and offered me a small smile.

Then he began to change, his scales lightened until they were paler than mine. His sail and frill whitened to a pale gray. Shrinking in size till he was smaller than me. His expression changed from one of curious concern to one of absolute terror. It was at that moment that I realized I was no longer hugging him but pinning him on his back to the floor.

"Lightscale," I whispered, recognizing the Síren from back when I was a youngling. He whimpered at his name. I stared at him for a minute before releasing him. The youngling immediately flipped over and darted for the exit. "Lightscale?" I called. He hesitated, one hand on the exit. "I'm sorry for chasing you off. I understand now that you were just looking for a home. A place to belong to." Lightscale turned and smiled at me.

Suddenly he looked bigger, more muscular, all of his scales grown in. No longer a youngling.

"It's ok, it's all just part of our nature right? Besides-" he flexed an arm, letting the arm-fin to flare out. "I think I turned out alright, don't you think?" he asked with a mischievous grin before fading away.

I blinked and then scrubbed aggressively at my face with my hands.

"Cracking ice, he's good looking, why oh why did I chase him off?" I lay there on the floor for a while bemoaning about how I could've potentially snagged him as a mate if I'd not chased him off.

"Sáo?" I froze, I know that voice. I pushed myself off the floor and turned around. "What are you doing there? I told you to come help me with this order." There was a Síren at the desk holding a half carved chunk of ice, a Síren with dark gray scales and blue/green frill and sail. Frostsight.

I swam over to the desk and Frostsight passed me the sculpture, "Hold it still." I clung to the sculpture, staring at her. I hadn't really thought about how Frostsight might've reacted to me coming back. Especially since the whole point of leaving was to find your own place to live and stay there. While I hadn't really been expecting her to react a certain way, I definitely hadn't expected her to act as though I was still a Youngling and still lived with her. My hand spasmed and I gripped the sculpture harder. Crack!

"Sáo!"

I glanced down, I'd broken the sculpture.

I winced. "Sorry Mum."

Frostsight tugged at her frill, something she always did when she was annoyed. "Honestly, what is up with you recently? Getting caught by humans, trusting a mermaid, now this?"

I froze. "What was that?"

Frostsight took the broken sculpture. "I said you broke my customer's sculpture."

"No, before that."

"Oh? I said you trusted a mermaid." She turned and tossed the ruined sculpture into the bowl.

My sail prickled, "How did you know about that?"

Frostsight chuckled, and I noticed her scales starting to ripple and change. "How did I know? Well of course I know, after all-" Frostsight's scales darkened from light gray to black, as she turned around to face me.

"I was there!" She screamed before lunging at me. I

103

froze in terror. Echo? She slammed into me sending us both tumbling.

"What happened to looking out for each other?!" Echo screamed. I shoved her off me and tried to dart away, but the exit out of the shop had disappeared. I felt the water shift behind me and quickly zipped to the side. Just in time for Echo to fly past me. I shot for the tunnel leading to the living quarters, but Echo grabbed my tail-fin and pulled me back towards her.

"What are you going to tell Larissa?! How will you explain to her that her master is dead?!" Echo cried. I smacked Echo with my tail-fin and wiggled away.

"I'll tell her the truth! I didn't mean for you to get killed, I didn't know you were down there!"

Echo spun around quickly, striking me with her tail and sending me tumbling. "Yet you got me killed anyway," she hissed. I shook my head looking for a way out, my gills opening and closing rapidly.

I can't fight her, I won't! I darted away. Up the tunnel, to the living space. Echo followed me. With a little trickery and some quick turns I dodged Echo's claws and shot back down the tunnel into the shop.

I remembered that the tunnel was opposite the wall with the shelves just in time. I turned quickly, just barely avoiding the shelves. But Echo didn't and crashed into the shelves, I winced as they shattered. Echo shuddered, but was dazed. I need to get out of here. I pressed my hands against the smooth wall that once had a doorway. Maybe it's an illusion. I took a deep breath, sniffing the water. I'd once read that illusions gave off a faint bitter scent.

All I could smell was a strong sweet scent. I scrunched up my nose. The smell was everywhere.

I spotted a flicker of pale purple in the water. Blood. I glanced over myself, not mine.

There was a soft hiss behind me and I turned. Echo approached me in a circling manner, I copied her. Echo shrieked at me as we both circled. I watched her warily, paused and blinked in confusion. Echo suddenly had a deep cut along her side.

Was that there before? Even as I watched her, more cuts appeared on Echo's body. Gradually turning the water around her purple. "Echo," I said slowly. "You're bleeding, you've got injuries on your chest, arms, and side. If you keep moving, you risk worsening them."

Echo gave me a cold grin. "I know." She swam closer, menacingly.

"Echo please stop! You're hurt!" I begged.

Echo hissed at me, a thin stream of blood floating out of her mouth. "And who's fault is that?!" she snarled, before choking and coughing.

I reached out a hand to help steady her, but she slapped it away. Echo tackled me again, and pinned me down.

"She's not dead!" Echo screamed.

I gasped and shot off the ground. Oh it was just a dream. I shook myself. Weird dream.

I heard a rattling sound. Oh the human's back. I approached the clear-wall. Sure enough the human had entered the room and was sitting on the large sitting spot. It grabbed at its head. Is it hurt? I pressed a hand to the clear-wall. The old human –who I'd started referring to as Silvery due to the grey/white tuft of fur on its head– sat there for a very long time. Maybe it hurts.

After a while Silvery approached my tank and stared at me. It watched me for a full minute before turning and walking towards the desk. Silvery then pulled a little rectangular thing out of nowhere and started chattering to it. What's it doing? I got closer to the clear-wall to peer curiously at Silvery. But its back was to me so I couldn't see much. Silvery spoke to the rectangular thing for a few more minutes before leaving the room. And there goes the only interesting thing about this place. I curled up to rest.

Wait. Did I eat supper?

I jerked awake, five humans had suddenly barged into the room carrying a container that looked eerily familiar. "Hey, Silvery. What's going on?" I didn't really expect an answer and I didn't get one. I swam in a circle. "It's not breakfast time yet."

The five new humans put up some weird things next to the tank and three of the humans climbed up them to reach the top of my tank. I coiled up and looked up at the humans. The other two humans had passed them some long hooked rods. The three humans started using the rods to reach down to me. I waited until they were just about to hook me before swimming away.

The humans ended up chasing me across the tank several times until one of them seemed to have the bright idea of using a net to catch me.

I grumbled softly as the humans slowly hauled me out of the tank. Once they had me out they shoved me into the little container, and closed it. Well. That didn't take long.

The sound of human voices woke me up. I yawned and stretched as much as the tiny container allowed. I could feel the container being moved around before being roughly dropped. I yelped as my sail got squished. There was a human moving around outside the container, after a moment the human started to open the top of the container. Sending a blinding beam of light into my eyes I squinted at the light, a large human leaned over the container blocking the light. I hissed softly and arched my back. The human didn't seem to care and reached into the container picking me up. I went limp, trying to make it hard for the human. But there was no reaction from the large human, it only adjusted its grip and kept going. The human brought me over to a low tank on the ground, it dropped me into the tank before leaving.

I looked around, there wasn't anything special around. There was a large cage next to my tank, but I couldn't see if anything was in it.

Well this is a surprise. A calm voice said.

I whipped my head around. "Who said that?!" I could hear something move in the cage and a creature appeared in my line of view.

I gasped, "It's you!" The vampire me and Echo had helped once just after we had arrived on Earth was there.

The vampire dipped his head, *we meet again.*

I grinned, "It's nice to see a familiar face, even if I don't know it very well."

The vampire swished his tail. *Indeed, perhaps I will finally be able to repay that debt I owe you.*

I shook my head in horror. "Debt? No! You don't owe me anything, it was simply the right thing to do!"

He reached out and patted my head. *Without your help I would've surely drowned.* He tilted his head. *I hope you are not trying to belittle a sacred vampire custom, are you?* He asked.

I flattened my sail. "No! I wasn't trying to-"

It's alright, I'm joking. We do not have any custom like that. His eyes twinkled with amusement. *I owe you simply because it is the right thing to do.*

I exhaled in relief, some supernaturals were very insistent on their customs and could be easily offended if said customs were neglected or insulted.

"What's your name anyway? I don't think you told me."

My name is Kippa.

I smiled. "I'm Sáo."

I swam in a circle a couple times. It would be nice if I could just sleep until something exciting happens, but I'm not tired. Echo flashed across my mind and I chuffed.

That Síren could sleep almost anywhere, just had a two hour long nap but nothing interesting was happening or about to happen? Back to sleep she went. Unless it was time for her patrol, then she was awake and ready.

I coiled up and sighed. "It's so boring just staying here. Could you tell me about your homeland?"

Kippa peered in the tank at me. *Why?*

I shrugged. "Curiosity. I've read a lot of ice slabs, but I don't know much about your kind."

Kippa blinked but didn't say anything.

"Hey, vampires like learning and knowledge right? Tell me about your kind and I'll tell you about mine."

Kippa's eyes widened. *Really?*

I smirked. Got him. "Of course!"

Kippa repositioned the way he was sitting. *Well in that case, ask away.*

I took a deep breath. "So I read somewhere that all of your young are born in the same place and raised by your elders. Is that true? And that you have a great burial place for all of your dead?"

Kippa crossed his front legs. *You are thinking of Tassta, the vampire city. Both of your questions are correct, all of our young are raised by the elders.*

I tilted my head. "So you don't ever get to meet your parents?"

Not always, but it is alright.

"Are there only elders and younglings in Tassta?"

It is mostly elders and younglings, there are a few adults that live there but they are all students.

"Students?"

Yes, the only vampires that are allowed to stay after becoming adults are those in training to work at The Temple. I closed my eyes and dug through my memories. "The Temple. Is that the one for your Great Ancestor?" I asked.

Yes, I was actually in training to work there before I was sent to Earth.

"Really?" I gasped softly, "that's so cool!" Kippa turned his head bashfully. "Does that mean you've been taught all the lore and history about your kind?"

Yes.

"Amazing, could you tell me?"

Kippa started disappearing from view. *I can.*

"Where are you going? Don't be embarrassed! You haven't even asked me any questions yet!"

Kippa shot back into view. *I forgot about that.* Well that sure got his attention. *Right, so I wanted to know-* The sound of something slamming cut him off. The large human was back, it stomped over to my tank. I hissed at it. I could see a second human approaching Kippa's cage.

The large human grabbed me and started taking me away. "Sorry Kippa, I think we're gonna have to resume this conversation later," I called. Kippa nodded and turned his attention back to the human near his cage.

The large human carried me for a while, enough time for me to start to worry if I was going to suffocate. But before

109

long the human brought me into a large room. I looked around, trying to see my new surroundings when suddenly the large human dropped me. I squealed as I fell, fortunately I didn't have too far to fall and ended up landing in water. I dunked my head underwater to take a breath.

The human had dropped me into a pit that was in the room. I swam around the pit. Nothing interesting here. Hearing the sound of scuffling I tried to peer out of the pit. Are they putting something else in the pit? I spotted something white and suddenly Kippa was sent tumbling into the pit. He looked startled, I snickered at his expression.

"What? Can't handle a little water?"

Kippa clacked his teeth, lifting a paw out of the water he shook it aggressively before putting it back down again. *I do not mind water. I just prefer to stay out of it.*

I then noticed the humans watching us from outside the pit seemed angry. "What's got their tails in a twist?"

Kippa followed my gaze. *They want us to fight. I've read about this, humans will sometimes force other creatures to fight each other for entertainment.*

I looked over at Kippa. "But what if we refuse to fight?"

Kippa didn't answer.

"Kippa? I don't want to fight you."

Nor I you.

One human –the large one from before– started yelling at us. It looked angry. When neither of us reacted the human pulled out something that looked like a piece of carved grey ice and pointed it at us.

"Kippa what's it doing?"

Kippa moved to stand over me, never looking away from the human. His head lowered and his long tail lashed. *Sáo. Look away.*

The human pointed the thing at Kippa.

"Kippa?"

My debt is paid.

CRACK

I screamed, covering my frill at the loud noise. Kippa jumped up slightly and then collapsed. I clutched at my frill, all I could hear was a loud ringing sound. I opened an eye, Kippa had collapsed on top of me and was now partly pinning me down. I wiggled out from under him.

"Kippa?" I whispered. "Kippa wake up." I shook his shoulder. "Kippa please." I could hear the human approaching from behind. "I don't want to be alone again." There was a splash from right behind me, I whipped around with a snarl. The human had jumped down into the pit and was pointing the thing at me now. I raised my sail and flared out my frill, trying to look as big as possible. I met the human's eyes and growled. Its eyes were cold and uncaring. I arched my back.

Click.

✦ *Chapter 10* ✦

✦ *Echo.* ✦

The human dropped me roughly into my tank. "Thanks for the ride, would it kill you to not drop me like a rotting carcass though?" As expected the human ignored me and stalked away to do humany things.

I glanced over at Moonhunter, he was curled up with his back to me. I sprawled out as much as my tank allowed me and started stacking the shedded scales that were scattered through my side of the tank. I had a stack of thirteen going when I looked up at Moonhunter, he hadn't moved a bit. He's probably asleep.

Did you ever have a sibling? I jumped slightly at the sound of his voice in my head. I blinked and thought back to when I lived with the Elder. I had a vague memory of the Great Mother saying something about siblings.

"I'm not sure. I think I did but they died before they left their nests."

Hmm. Moonhunter swished his tail but didn't turn to face me.

How... did you know Sáo anyway?

I fiddled with a loose scale on my arm, "We were put together in a cave that brought us to Earth."

Hm?

I pulled off the loose scale. "Shortly after we landed on Earth, we ended up living together in a cave."

Moonhunter snorted, *I find it hard to believe a wild-born would agree to sharing territory.*

I tossed the scale away and scratched at my arm again. "I didn't, not at first. But your sister could be very persuasive, it probably also helped that I had gill-rot at the time and she conveniently knew how to treat it."

You stayed with her after you were healed. A statement, not a question.

"Yup, she was convinced we were friends and I guess it got to me."

Moonhunter made a soft snorting sound. *She always was very persistent.* Neither of us said anything for a little while.

I scratched at my side again, huffing when yet another scale fell off.

Problem?

I glanced at him out of the corner of my eye. "Why do you care?"

I don't, but I'm bored.

I picked off a loose scale. "Scale issues."

Hm? He rolled over to look. *Could be wiggle worms.*

"What."

He picked up a scale that had drifted over to his side of the tank, he examined it for a moment before tossing it back to my side of the tank. *Little parasites that burrow under the skin and feed off of your blood. They can make your scales fall off.*

"WHAT." I immediately began checking all the spots where scales fell off.

There was a soft snuffling sound. I looked back at the

other Síren, he was staring at me with a strange expression on his face, he placed a hand over his mouth.

Wiggle worms don't exist. I made it up.

"I'm going to murder you." I glared at him as he snuffled softly again.

Judging from what I can see, you're growing your glow-scales.

"Really?" I drawled. Not tricking me this time.

Yes. You get them as you start to transition from being a wanderling to an adult. They're supposed to help attract potential mates.

"Fascinating."

I'm serious, didn't you ever notice the glow-scales on your parent? Any scale patterns?

I closed my eyes to think. I thought about the Elder, I wasn't really sure but it was possible he'd had a faint gray patterning along his side. But I'd never paid attention to it since it hadn't seemed very significant.

You don't believe me do you?

"Nope."

Moonhunter sighed and wiggled closer to the bars. *Come here, I'll show you.* I approached warily. *See?* He traced a line along his side. *Glow-scales.*

I blinked, sure enough there was a pale green pattern along his side.

"They don't look very glowy."

Moonhunter rolled his eyes, *of course they don't. I didn't activate them.*

"What do they look like activated then?" Moonhunter didn't respond and for a moment I thought that he'd been bluffing, then suddenly, the tank was illuminated with a faint green light. *Still don't believe me?*

I exhaled softly, it was quite pretty. I looked up at

Moonhunter's face. He had a very smug expression on. I turned my back to him and his light. "Nope."

Oh come on, you can literally see my scales glowing!

I glanced back at him. "I know. You're just annoying."

Moonhunter huffed. *You're welcome for solving your scale shedding problem. Your glow-scales should finish growing in about a month or so. You're probably going to be itchy where the scales are shedding.*

Ignoring him I curled up on my uninjured side, which unfortunately left me facing Moonhunter. I rubbed my side where the creature's venom had splashed, it stung.

Hurting?

I nodded, "Yeah."

Moonhunter repositioned himself. *What'd you fight?*

"Huh?"

Moonhunter rolled his eyes, *what did the humans put in the pit with you?*

Understanding the question I told him about the creature I'd faced.

Hm. Sounds like you fought a basilisk. That's pretty lucky for your first time, my first round they tossed me in with a werewolf. Crazy thing ripped out part of my sail. I eyed him doubtfully, "A werewolf. Worse than something that has acidic venom dripping from its fangs, and can freeze you in place just by looking at its eyes?"

Moonhunter hesitated. *Well, I guess fighting a basilisk for the first time can be challenging. But after the first one they're fairly easy.*

He's shockingly chatty when he wants to be.

"You've fought a lot of basilisks then?"

Moonhunter flicked his frill. *A few.*

"Any other wisdom to offer?"

Basilisks may seem tough —and they can be— but once

115

you've figured out what to do with them it's pretty simple. Sure, Basilisks have that rather annoying ability to make you freeze with fear if you look them in the eyes. Blinding or gouging out their eyes solves that problem.

"How would you blind them?" I asked.

Basilisks aren't very smart, all they do is charge at whatever's in front of their snouts. I once tricked a Basilisk into repeatedly charging into the pit walls so many times it actually knocked itself out for a solid minute which gave me a chance to attack it, so that works.

Werewolves are tricky, they can be unpredictable and that's what makes them dangerous.
Unicorns are just plain crazy, I wouldn't advise going against one. Chimeras and manticores, now those are dangerous. I've never fought one and if I'm lucky I never will have to.

"You know about them though."

Yes, I once did some research on them while I was still on Neptune. Moonhunter yawned and coiled up with his back to me, *going to sleep now, don't bother me.*

And so much for being chatty.

I thought quietly for a moment. "What about vampires? Ever fought one of those?"

Hm? No, I haven't. Why?

I scratched my arm again, "Me and Sáo once came across one."

Moonhunter turned around to look at me, *you fought it?*

I shook my head. "No, we saved it." At Moonhunter's questioning look I elaborated.

"When we were just leaving the cave –tunnel? thing?– that brought us to Earth we found a vampire stuck with his tail pinned under some rocks. Sáo decided to help him since vampires can't breathe underwater."

116

That sounds like her. Moonhunter quieted down and when I checked, he was asleep. I yawned and coiled up to sleep as well.

-✦-

I felt the water ripple and peeked out of the tank. The muscular human was back. Seriously? Me and Moonhunter had been telling each other funny stories of ridiculous things we'd seen Sáo do, it'd felt nice to learn a little more about her past. I was also starting to almost enjoy talking with Moonhunter. We'd been chatting for so long I'd forgotten to be sarcastic while speaking to him. It seemed to be easier to like him when he was talking about Sáo. I tensed up, ready for the human. Moonhunter watched curiously. But the muscular human only approached my tank, and took something out of a basket it held and dropped it in.

"Oh."

Moonhunter chuckled. *It's not taking you to the pit, you were just there.* The muscular human put down the basket and moved over to his tank. *It's coming for me.*

Moonhunter hissed at the human as it snagged him with the rope on a rod. Since I wasn't the one being grabbed I could see how the human actually did it. Once the rope was around Moonhunter's neck the muscular human jerked the rod and the rope tightened. Moonhunter made a soft choking noise and thrashed. The human latched the rod into a hook-thing on Moonhunter's tank and began wrapping him up in the leaf-wrap. Once Moonhunter was all wrapped up, the human –still pinning him– unlatched the rod and removed the rope from his neck. The human tossed the rod aside and picked Moonhunter up. It struggled a bit while picking him up. Moonhunter sensed the human's weakness and started trying to wiggle out of the wrap. I laughed as the human struggled to keep hold of him.

I noticed then that the human was surprisingly large and not just in muscle. It was about the same size as Moonhunter and I, which I thought was strange. I'd never paid attention to the human that I'd attacked back when I'd been with Tulva, but I did remember that it was definitely smaller than me, barely a tail-length in size. After a few more minutes the human managed to grab Moonhunter firmly and started walking away. I spotted Moonhunter wiggle his head free enough to peek out of the wrap.

I gave him a little wave to which he responded by pulling a hand free and offering me a rather rude gesture in return. I cackled evilly.

"Good luck!" I called.

I ate the thing the muscular human dropped in –it was a piece of cod, my absolute least favorite type of fish, but I was hungry so I had no choice– and coiled up to rest. I dozed for a while before waking up to the sound of a human approaching. I yawned. The muscular human appeared over my tank.

"I hope you're here to give me more food cause that little thing you gave me earlier barely counts as a snack."

The muscular human dropped the wrap on me and wrapped me up while lifting me in one smooth motion.

Wait. The human started carrying me away from my tank. "Wait. Nooooo!" I wailed. "I was in the perfect position!"

The human hauled me over to the pit again. This time when I was tossed in, I was able to control my landing better and avoid smacking into the ground chest first. I growled grumpily, it had taken forever for me to get in that spot and the human just had to ruin it. I looked around and shook my head. Not taking me to the pit, I was just there, well how do you explain this you aggravating city-born?

I looked around for whatever creature the humans wanted me to fight but the pit was empty. I looked around, this wasn't the same pit. My gills started stinging. I dunked my head underwater. The water's much shallower, just over an arm-length, barely high enough to cover me. I flattened my sail and twisted my tail so that my tail-fin was flat against the ground. Even lying like that there was barely a hand's width of water covering me. I spotted something near the edge of the pit out of the corner of my eye. It looked vaguely like a human, it had most of the basic human shape except for the massive, glowing things where its shoulders were supposed to be.

I stared in horror at the creature for a minute, then I realized it was a human with two slightly glowing creatures on its shoulders. The human raised something to its mouth and made a loud whistling noise. The two creatures lifted off of the human's shoulders. I froze in place.

What. The glowing creatures flew around the pit once before perching on the edge of the pit above my head.

"Oh, how interesting." One of them said, I swiveled my neck to look up at the strange creatures above my head.

"They talk," I muttered.

The creature on the left puffed up in annoyance. "*They talk.* Well of course we talk!"

"I apologize for my sister dear. See we've never fought another intelligent supernatural before." The creature on the right said. I tilted my head. The creature on the right adjusted its grip on the edge of the pit.

"How did you do that?" I asked.

"Do what, dear?"

I waved a hand around the pit. "You flew."

"Well we can fly because we're phoenixes dear. We have wings you see." The creature –phoenix– on the right raised its wings.

Huh. There was another whistle.

"Well, I am sorry to do this to you dear. It has been nice talking to you and we don't get to talk with other supernaturals often."

I blinked. "What are you sorry for?"

The phoenix on the left raised its wings. "For killing you of course."

With that both phoenixes lifted their wings and were suddenly enveloped by fire. They launched off the edge of the pit and dove towards me. I reeled backwards and raised my arms to protect my face. There was a flash of pain across my right forearm as they swooped by me. I turned around so I could see them. They're fast, I would have to keep my eyes on them.

There was a soft rattling sound, I looked up, the humans had pulled some sort of web over the pit. I hadn't noticed that last time. The phoenixes flew around the pit, just under the web. It's keeping them inside.

I watched the phoenixes, a memory of a voice flickering through my mind. *Beware of fire, Echo.* Mother, I really wish you could've told me what to do if I had to deal with fire.

Several times the phoenixes swooped by me, testing me for any weaknesses. I watched them passively, I knew that the second I tried to engage one of them the other would attack me from behind.

As one of the phoenixes swooped by me, I grabbed it but quickly let go with a shriek when pain shot through both of my hands. I checked my hands, they were stinging with pain and the scales looked slightly damaged.

How did it..? The phoenix fluttered up towards the other, then they both dived at me. My arms still remembered the pain from the first time they dived at me, so I quickly dipped back in the water flattening myself against the ground. I turned my head to see. Just before the phoenixes hit the water they swooped up and glided over me. I popped up out of the water.

Why didn't they attack? I wondered, the water isn't that deep. I hesitated, the water. When the phoenixes swooped at me again I smacked one at the water. It hit the water and immediately splashed up into the air again.

Can't handle a little water huh? I smiled. I can use that.

One of the phoenixes flared out its wings and sent out a burst of fire that I barely managed to dodge. Oh right, they're basically made of fire. The phoenixes swooped at me, the first one flew around my head, shrieking and sending out bursts of fire.

Suddenly a sharp burst of pain shot through my side, and I felt myself being lifted out of the water. I turned, the second phoenix had grabbed me and was now trying to carry me. I thrashed and it lost its grip. The phoenixes flew off again and started swooping around my head.

I growled. Ok, I'm tired of this. I grabbed one of the phoenixes out of the air, ignoring the pain in my hands and the other phoenix which was angrily swooping at my head. I plunged the phoenix in the water, it shrieked and thrashed but I held it down. The fire on its body started to die out, and bubbles flooded out of its mouth. I was killing it.

The second phoenix flew up to me and grabbed my face with its claws. It flared its wings and there was a bright flash of light. I screamed and clutched at my face, my eyes stung. I could hear a faint splashing noise just in front of me. I hissed in pain and slowly removed my hands from my eyes, everything looked blurry and strange.

I could see the one phoenix lifting its friend out of the water. I shook my head, trying to clear the fuzz from my eyes. For a moment all of us recovered, before continuing the fight.

Every chance I got, I grabbed one of the phoenixes and plunged them in the water, and they in turn sent fireballs at me and scratched me with their sharp claws. I couldn't hold them under the water for more than a few seconds, but slowly and surely the frequent dunkings began to wear on them.

I glanced down at my hands, the scales on the palms had been completely seared away revealing the now pale and leathery skin. I grimaced at the damage.

I don't know how many more times my hands will be able to handle that trick. I thought.

I twitched my fingers, they didn't hurt anymore but they were quite stiff.

I watched as the phoenixes mock swooped over my head again, they were moving slower. They're tired. The phoenixes had been at a disadvantage from the start.

The entire pit floor was covered in water, meaning that if the phoenixes got tired they couldn't land and they couldn't leave to rest either because of the web over the pit. I smiled, I on the other hand could simply flatten my sail and sink to the bottom if I wanted a break since the phoenixes wouldn't touch the water unless it was to help pull each other out.

One more time. I thought. Waiting for the perfect moment, I lunged up out of the water. Grabbing both of the phoenixes by their feet, I pulled them down to the water. I was tired, but so were they and while I didn't have the strength to completely submerge them, I could pull them down enough that everytime they flapped their wings they got splashed.

Suddenly there was a loud whistle, I let go of the phoenixes and covered my frill. The phoenixes, seeing their chance, fluttered away. I watched them, the web was being pulled off the pit by a couple humans. The phoenixes swooped up past the half-removed web and back to the human they'd been perching on before. I grimaced, rubbing my frill. Ouch...

There was another loud whistle and I shrieked in pain, covering my frill again to protect it from the piercing sound. When the sound was over, I looked around growling, waiting for a possible trick.

"You can calm down now dear, the humans have decided you're the winner." One of the phoenixes called to me.

I'm the winner? But I didn't kill them. Past the slight ringing in my frill, I could hear humans yelling from where they were around the pit. I couldn't tell if they sounded angry or happy. I slumped down into the water, it was no longer cool and refreshing. I took a couple deep breaths, the warm water irritated my gills. I hope I don't get gill-rot from this. I barely noticed as the muscular human slid down into the pit and wrapped me up in the leaf wrap once again.

The human brought me back to my tank and dropped me in. I glanced over at the tank on the other side of the bars. Moonhunter was not here. Maybe his fight wasn't over yet. I sank to the bottom of the tank and began checking all of my injuries.

There were fairly deep gashes along my side from where one of the phoenixes had tried to pick me up. I gingerly prodded at one of the gashes and shuddered in pain. My arms and hands were also injured. My arms were tinged purple.

I poked my arm. The skin that I could see paled at my touch and hurt quite a bit. I turned my attention to my hands, they didn't hurt and that worried me. When I'd grabbed a phoenix the first time it had hurt a lot, but the more I'd grabbed the phoenixes and shoved them underwater, the less it'd hurt. I tried to wiggle my fingers, they barely twitched, that can't be good.

My frill flicked, a human was coming. Oh come on. A human appeared over my tank. I didn't recognize it. I growled softly. The human reached into my tank and grabbed one of my arms. I shrieked as it grabbed my arm right where the fire had got me and yanked my arm away.

I backed away from the human as far away as I could. The human reached for me again, I growled and not wanting to use my hands, I bit the human. The human cried out pulling its hand away, it backed off and called out.

Shortly after the muscular human appeared. The two humans spoke to each other for a moment before coming back to my tank. The muscular human reached in with the rod. I hissed but there wasn't much I could do. The muscular human snagged me, this time instead of just pinning me to the ground with the one rod, it grabbed two other rods from somewhere and used those to pin me down further. I tried to squirm away but the muscular human was strong and I was tired. It called to the other human, who approached and grabbed my right arm. I hissed in pain, my arm stinging. The other human began wrapping something around my right arm. I hissed and cried but the muscular human kept me from moving. Once it was done with my right arm the human grabbed my other arm and started giving it the same treatment. When it was done with my arms it turned to my side. The other human poked and prodded at my side for a minute.

Eventually the humans released me and I moved as far away from them as possible. I examined my arms to see what they did. The human had tightly wrapped something that looked a bit like a seaweed bandage around my injuries. I touched the wraps suspiciously and glanced up at the humans. The muscular human had left, but the new human was still there. It watched me for a little while before leaving.

Weird humans.

 *Sáo.*

I lay coiled up in my tank. For some reason the human changed its mind, instead of killing me it grabbed and dragged me all the way back, not even bothering to carry me. When we reached my tank, it tossed me in.

I looked up, Kippa's tank was empty. Of course it was, he was dead. I heard a soft clatter and a human approached Kippa's empty cage. The human went into the cage and began cleaning it. It cleaned for a few minutes before leaving. I watched it sadly.

Once the humans left I had nothing to do. I looked down at my scales, pure white. Almost. I traced the odd scales on my arm. The odd scales were a bunch of scales that didn't resemble the others. Instead of white they were a dark gray. Echo had once called them reverse stars. I shivered, Echo. Someone else I'd known and gotten killed.

I looked up, a human was approaching my tank. I peeked up, curious. The human was awkwardly carrying a massive bucket, a smaller bucket, and cleaning supplies. It placed the bucket and cleaning supplies next to my tank and started pulling at something next to my tank. I peered over the edge of my tank to see. I hadn't really paid attention to

125

what was on this side of my tank since it was on the opposite side from where Kippa used to be. The human was trying to pull a sheet off of a large box-shaped thing yanked hard at the sheet and it flew off revealing another tank. It cleaned out the tank before picking up the massive bucket and dumping all –well most– of the water into it. I looked in the new tank, other than water there wasn't anything in it.

A little while later the human was back again, this time with a friend. The pair were carrying something large and wrapped up. The humans walked over to the other tank and placed the thing in it, releasing it from the wrap and walking away. Oh, it's a Síren. Using my arms to support myself I pulled myself up out of my tank further to get a better look. The other Síren was clearly injured. Part of his sail was ripped off, there were deep gashes along his side and arms. Did he even win?

Uncertain how to react, I raised my sail and hissed. The other Síren reacted to that, pushing himself off the floor and swinging his head from side to side. I noticed that there was a strange wrap around his head that covered his eyes. He can't see me, I realized. I reached out of my tank and tapped his tank wall. The other Síren's head whipped around to face me. He hissed back at me but he sounded hesitant, and afraid.

The other Síren kept feeling around his tank, must be hard being unable to see. I watched him for a little while. He looked a bit familiar but I didn't know why. I examined him, light gray scales, darker gray sail. Same as Moonhunter, for a moment I stared at the other Síren considering how likely the chances were that I was being held captive with my brother. The same brother I'd ditched like a coward when those Síren had come to take us. I shook my head, no can't be him, gray was one of the most common colors in

126

the city. It was probably a different Síren that was similar in color. I considered talking to him, to see if he responded or not. There were a lot of gray-scaled Síren in the city, but I doubted there were many mute Síren with gray scales. I was about to say hello then hesitated, what if it was him? What if he hated me for leaving him? What if the humans made me fight him?

My gills screamed for water, I lowered myself back down into the tank feeling like a coward, too scared to find out if it was Moonhunter or not. My arm grazed against the tank's stone walls, irritating the scales. I scratched my arm out of reflex, and blinked in surprise when a scale came off. I looked at my arm to find where the scale came from. I found another loose scale and pulled it off. I examined the scale. Now what would cause my scales to fall off? I poked at the spot where the scales came from. I could tell that there were more scales that felt slightly loose, but I didn't pull them out.

Oh, these must be my glow-scales growing in. I thought, coiling up. I should rest, never know when the humans might decide to toss me in that pit again. I gotta be ready to kill, otherwise they'll kill me. I closed my eyes to sleep.

I saw the human, standing right in front of me. Pointing that strange thing at my head. Kippa lying in the shallow water next to me, his pale blue blood mixing with the water staining my hands.

My eyes snapped open. I looked at my hands, they weren't blue. The human wasn't here. Kippa was gone. I was alone, I covered my face with my hands and sobbed.

✛ *The kraken, the witch, and the hippocampus.* ✛

Larissa stared up at the beam, after going back to the beach they'd stayed there for a little while for Dei to take a break before heading back out to follow the beam. The beam had led them pretty far. The trio had been following it across the ocean for around ten days, before it turned abruptly towards land. The beam then led them up a river for a little while before turning off onto land.

Dei clambered off Squishy's back and stretched, "Ah, solid ground."

<Now what do we do? Me and Squishy can't go on land!> Larissa cried, swimming in circles.

Dei chuckled at her. She's like a worried dog. "No worries, I have a spell."

Squishy blinked skeptically. <Do you have a spell for everything?>

Dei laughed, "I don't have a spell for world peace." Noticing their confused expressions, he winced. "Ah sorry, just a joke."

<Do you need anything for the spell?> Squishy asked.

Dei nodded. "Yeah most of the stuff I need is on land though, let me check."

Dei began rummaging through a bag that Larissa could have sworn wasn't there before.

<Where'd you get that?> She asked.

Dei glanced at her, "Get what?"

She pointed her snout at the bag, <That bag.>

Dei looked down at the bag as if he hadn't realized he was holding it. "This? I've had it the whole time."

Larissa blinked. <You didn't have it when we went to that boat thing.>

Dei shrugged, "True, I actually didn't get a chance to pick it up when you and Squishy came back to get me so I ended up leaving it on the beach. One of the main reasons why I wanted to go back to the beach after was because I'd left my bag there. Aha! Found it." Dei pulled something out of his bag.

Larissa leaned closer, <What is that?>

Dei held the thing up, "It's a book! I use it to keep track of all my spells." Dei flicked through the book, trying to find the spell. "Ah here it is," he squinted at the page, before looking around at his surroundings. "Ok I think I can find pretty much everything I need, Squishy do you think you could find me some oysters? I'm going to need them." Squishy disappeared back into the ocean with a flick of a tentacle.

Dei crouched down and dug a shallow hole attached to the river and lined it with rocks, he let river water flow in and made a little rock wall between the hole and the river.

Larissa watched him curiously. <What are you doing?> She asked.

Dei chuckled, "You'll see." He straightened, "Wait here, I'll be back." Larissa watched as Dei disappeared into the underbrush.

Larissa waited, she waited patiently, semi-patiently, and impatiently. Finally Dei returned carrying a bunch of plants.

Larissa dipped her head in and out of the water. <What are those for?>

"The spell," Dei replied vaguely, sitting down.

Squishy reappeared, <is twenty enough?> He tossed the oysters onto the riverside.

Dei scooped up the oysters, "Twenty? Yeah thanks." Dei put the oysters into the hole. Then Dei's left hand began to glow with a strange light. Larissa and Squishy watched fascinated, as Dei plunged his glowing hand into the hole with the oysters.

129

The water began to hiss and steam. Dei kept his hand in the water for several minutes before pulling his hand out. He noticed them watching him. "What?"

<Why'd you do that?> Squishy asked, <they were perfectly fine.>

Dei squinted at them, "I can't eat oysters raw. I'd get sick."

He took his bundle of plants and spread them out a bit. "Ok, spell time. I'll start with you, Squishy. Be warned, the new form I'm giving you can't breathe underwater, so you might want to pull yourself into the shallow water." Squishy wiggled into the shallow water.

Dei closed his eyes and began to chant. Larissa shivered, for some reason every time Dei did that she got a weird chill. Squishy began to shudder.

<Squishy? Are you ok?> Larissa asked, concerned. There was a bright flash of light from Squishy, and when it faded, he was completely changed.

<I don't think I like this,> Squishy said, laying on his side in the water.

Dei opened his eyes and grinned at him. "Just try to get up and get used to walking around, I need a break anyway," Dei said. He reached into the hole and took out a now open oyster. Squishy got to his feet and Dei watched him carefully.

It was his first time casting that spell and he wanted to be sure he did it right. Horse-Squishy looked pretty normal, other than the fact he still had eight legs. He wasn't purple anymore, now grey although he still had a faint purple shimmer to him but it wasn't very noticeable. "Hm. Other than the eight legs I think I did pretty good."

Dei brought the oyster to his mouth. He sucked it into his mouth and swallowed it as fast as he could. Dei made a face, "Bleh, seafood." He tossed aside the empty shell and picked up another oyster and ate it. Dei shuddered.

<If you don't like it why are you eating it?>

Dei swallowed a third oyster. "Gotta replenish my energy, and my bag's out of snacks. So-" he eyed the oysters, "I have to eat oysters."

<You have to eat to get more energy?>

Larissa thought back to when they had been back at the beach, she was pretty sure she'd seen Dei aggressively eating something while they were there.

Dei ate another oyster, "Sleeping also helps but we don't have time for me to take a nap right now."

Dei managed to eat five more oysters. Larissa watched him, trying to smother her laughter, she thought his reaction to oysters was hilarious.

Larissa looked over at the herbs, a weird smelling steam was rising off of the herbs.

"Gah." Dei began smacking the herbs. He kept smacking them until there was no more steam.

"Ok, that's enough of a break." He moved back to his original position, closed his eyes and started to chant.

Half way through, Dei peeked an eye open. Larissa was impatiently swimming in circles again. He smiled remembering the border collie he once had as a kid. That dog had followed him everywhere. He closed his eyes again and finished the spell. There was a bright flash of light, the feeling of being hit by a truck, and the spell was cast.

<Uhh Dei? I think the spell did something weird.>

Dei opened his eyes. "Ah, oops." Instead of turning Larissa into a horse like he'd meant to, he'd turned her into a dog, a border collie to be specific.

Larissa awkwardly climbed out of the water. <I thought you were turning me into a horse, like Squishy.>

"Sorry, I got distracted. You're a dog now." Dei flopped backward into the grass, closing his eyes with a sigh. "Larissa, could you come closer..?"

She wobbly trotted to Dei. Dei cracked open an eye. Dog-Larissa looked fairly normal, although the white patches on her looked blueish, her front paws were a bit hoof-like, and he was pretty sure he could see a hint on gills on her neck. But even though it wasn't the greatest job, it would trick anyone seeing her from a distance. He closed his eye again.

Squishy practiced walking around, it wasn't that he was new to moving around with eight limbs, it was that he was not used to moving around with eight limbs on land.

Squishy looked over at the oysters, he glanced at Dei. Squishy gave a horsey shrug and sneakily moved over to the oysters.

<Squishy don't eat those.>

<Too late.> Squishy said, crunching the last of the oysters.

Larissa huffed. Well we do need to get moving anyway. <Dei?>

No response.

<Dei.> Larissa nibbled his hand.

"Mmfh, what?"

<Don't we have to keep moving?>

"Oh. Right." He sat up and blinked blurrily, "Squishy get over here."

Squishy approached. <What do you need?>

"Crouch down for a moment." Squishy looked confused but did as Dei asked. Dei stood up and clambered onto Squishy's back.

<Can't walk on your own?> Squishy teased, getting to his feet.

"Poke fun at my tiredness and next time I'll turn you into a tadpole," Dei muttered, resting his head on Squishy's neck. "Don't let me fall off."

Larissa looked towards the direction the beam was leading, and pranced in place. <come on, come on let's go!>

The trio traveled over land for about a day, Dei slept most of the time. Larissa glanced up at Dei and sighed.

<What is it?> Squishy asked, awkwardly climbing over a fallen log.

<He's much more interesting when he's awake.>

Squishy snorted, <most creatures are.>

Larissa shook her head, <no, I mean he's fun to talk to.>

<And I'm not?>

<I talk to you all the time, plus all you think about is food.>

Squishy tossed his head. <That is not true. I only think of food most of the time.>

Larissa looked up at Dei again. <I'm waking him up.> She stood up wobbly on her hind legs and nudged Dei. He grumbled softly, but didn't react otherwise. She nibbled his hand before biting it.

"Ow," Dei said, stirring. "Did we find the humans yet?"

<Oh Dei you're awake!>

He glared at her and rubbed his hand. "I'm taking that as a no."

Larissa tilted her head at him, <you keep talking about the humans as if you're not one of them.>

Dei repositioned the way he was sitting and shrugged. "Well, I'm not quite a human. I'm a witch," he said with a yawn.

<What's a witch?>

"A witch is the hybrid child of a male human and a female elf. So I'm part human but not really human."

<Is that why you can cast spells?>

"Yup, normal humans can't use magic but elves, witches, and mages can. Did you wake me up just to ask me that?"

Larissa turned her attention away, <uhhmm.>

<Hey, look at that,> Squishy commented, distracting them both. Dei and Larissa turned to see what Squishy was looking at. Just through the trees in front of them was a strange building. They approached it hesitantly and peered at it from the safety of the undergrowth.

Dei, Larissa, and Squishy all stared up at the building.

<What is it?> Larissa asked.

"It's a warehouse. Wonder what one's doing all the way out here."

Squishy snorted. <Does it matter? Look, the beam is leading to it, that means Echo's inside right?> Dei nodded and slid off of Squishy's back.

Squishy pawed the ground, <then let's go.> Larissa and Squishy moved towards the warehouse.

"Wait!" Dei grabbed both of them. "Wait. Humans can be really dangerous."

<So?>

Dei took a deep breath. "So we shouldn't go in there all guns blazing, cause that'll just get us caught too."

<Why can't you just use that camouflage spell again?>

"That won't work in there. Camouflage only works if you have something to camouflage to. Plus how are we supposed to get your masters out of there? I know how big the average Síren is. I can't carry one let alone two."

<So then use the transforming spell on them.>

"That spell needs, like, six very specific plants to be cast and I highly doubt I could find them here."

<So then what are we supposed to do?> Larissa ran in a circle.

"I'll call my sisters, they're all in the SPF so they'll be able to help us." Dei pulled out his phone and tapped the screen.

Nothing happened. Larissa stood on her hind legs and leaned on him peering at his phone, <is it supposed to do something?>

Dei felt the tips of his ears redden. He tapped the screen aggressively several times before remembering he'd shut it down. He turned the phone on.

<Ooh.> Larissa said, leaning closer Squishy rested his chin on Dei's shoulder. Dei scooted away from the nosy creatures, and opened his contacts.

Oh wait, I don't think I told any of them that I left the cove. He scrolled through his options. Can't call Briar, she'll just teleport over here and drag me home before I can explain. Definitely don't call Cámí. Aril's out of the question. That just leaves Abÿss, she's the calmest anyway. Dei called Abÿss, the phone barely had time to ring before she answered.

"Hey Abÿss, so I know-"

"DEI, WHERE HAVE YOU BEEN?! YOU WERE SUPPOSED TO GO TO THE OCEAN TO PRACTICE YOUR FIRE MAGIC NOT DROP OFF THE FACE OF THE EARTH FOR TWO WEEKS! CÁMÍ WENT TO THE COVE WHERE YOU SAID YOU WERE GOING TO GO AND DO YOU KNOW WHAT HAPPENED?"

"I wasn't there?" Dei said in a meek voice.

"THAT'S RIGHT YOU WEREN'T THERE. DO YOU KNOW WHAT WE'VE WENT THROUGH TRYING

135

TO FIND YOU? WE COULDN'T EVEN FIND ANY OF YOUR THINGS FOR A SEEKING SPELL."

"D-does Mum know?" Dei asked, cringing slightly.

"YES AND SHE IS FURIOUS. YOU BETTER HAVE A REALLY GOOD EXCUSE FOR THIS."

At that point the other witch seemed to sense Dei's distress and calmed down. "Hey little sun, I'm sorry for yelling. I've just been really on edge these past couple weeks." Larissa nudged Dei's hand, reminding him why he called.

"Well you know how Briar and Aril have been complaining recently about not having any work to do?"

Abÿss was quiet for a moment, "Your disappearance gave them something to do."

Dei winced, "Well I found some work for them."

"What did you find, little sun?"

✦ *Echo.* ✦

The muscular human appeared over my tank. I looked up at it, hopeful. After the last fight I was starving, I technically hadn't eaten a proper meal since the humans had caught me. While a Síren could survive with little to no food for several weeks, that was only to conserve energy when searching for food. Now though, I desperately needed food. The human reached into my tank and grabbed me. I didn't struggle this time, no point. Once again the human once again hauled me to the pit. "Do you get tired of this?" I asked the human as it carried me. "Do you get tired of carrying me back and forth to the same places?" Of course the human didn't answer and tossed me into the pit.

I landed with a splash, there was more water in it than the last time. I looked around for my opponent. It was another Síren this time, I examined it. The other Síren looked a bit smaller than me and had what seemed to be white scales.

Those humans really are sick, pitting me against my own kind? Is this nothing but a game to them? Is my life just some form of entertainment? No matter, I will play this game, and I will win.

◇ *Sáo.* ◇

The large human was back, it picked me up. Back to the pit already. I thought. I glanced back at the other Síren, he was coiled up in a corner of his tank. I will not lose like he did. The human dropped me into the pit, I looked around. There wasn't anything else in the pit at the moment but I could tell by the way the watching humans were reacting that another creature was being brought to the pit.

A very muscular human approached the edge of the pit and tossed something in. Another Síren? I shook my head. doesn't matter, here it's kill or be killed. The other Síren was definitely larger than me, with scuffed looking black scales. The other Síren also seemed to be injured, it had human wraps on its arms and hands and I could see some sort of injury along its side. I tensed up, Echo once said that because I'm small I have to use every advantage I can find, and those look like advantages.

I tensed up, don't worry Kippa your sacrifice won't be in vain.

✦ *Chapter 11* ✦

✦ *Echo.* ✦

We circled, a dance of death. My arms were stinging in pain. Why so soon? I circled the other Síren. It's barely been a day since I fought those phoenixes. Didn't Moonhunter say that we usually get a break after fighting? Is this just my life now? Being tossed into the pit over and over again until I die? Why? Why do I have to do this? This isn't a fight over territory or food, it's meaningless.

The gashes in my side throbbed with pain every time I moved. While the humans had wrapped my arms, they had made no attempt to treat my side. I resisted the urge to glance at it, even if I win I doubt I'll survive.

◇ *Sáo.* ◇

I don't want to fight, I don't want to kill. But I want to live and fighting is the only way. Watching each other, we circled, the other Síren growled at me. Judging by the size, I'd say the other Síren was a male. I noticed that he kept shielding his right side. I could use that, I trembled, but how?! Fighting isn't my thing! Back in the city I didn't really get into fights, when I fought Echo back in the white cave I was mostly trying to flee from her. Even when we were living out in the ocean, the most violent thing I ever did was help Echo with the hunting.

He lunged at me, I screeched and spun away to the side. It was a mock lunge. The other Síren dove under me, moving his tail just enough that his tail-fin smacked me in the face. Rubbing my nose, the other Siren swooped back around

No wait, I had done some fighting. Echo found out that I had virtually no experience back when she was still recovering from gill-rot, and insisted on teaching me. I never really did get the hang of fighting another Síren, Echo said I'd be able to defend myself long enough for her to come help me. But Echo wasn't going to come save me, not this time. I watched the other Síren as he swam around me in circles, testing me, lunging towards me, trying to get me to panic. I took a deep breath and narrowed my eyes. Echo, I'll make you proud.

I charged at the other Síren, he raised his arms to shield himself. Just before we collided I veered to the right mock scratching his side, he darted away to the left and I followed him as he backed away.

✦ *Echo.* ✦

She's trying to corner me. I lashed out at the other Síren, she blocked my attack with a tail whip to the side. I cringed in pain and resisted the urge to press a hand to my side. The other Síren sensed my weakness and lunged at me. We wrestled for a minute, both of us trying to pin the other down. Finally I managed to grab her long enough to pin her down. I growled, ready to kill when I froze.

The other Síren stared up at me, her eyes watering.

For a moment I saw Sáo looking at me, her eyes full of silver tears. I hesitated, my hand resting on the other Síren's throat. She reached up and placed a hand against my neck, and then tore at my gills. I shrieked and jerked away, clutching at my gills. Pale purple blood mixed with the water.

I glowered at the other Síren. Crying to make me feel bad, what a dirty trick. I thought. I coughed, I was inhaling blood. That little slime-licker, she must have torn the gill membrane, now I was on a timer. I coughed again. I'd have to keep moving now, if I stopped, I'd start inhaling blood.

◇ *Sáo.* ◇

The other Síren had been about to strangle me but hesitated for some reason. I'd once read about a pressure point that Síren have in their necks just above the gills, supposedly pressing the point for a certain amount of time would cause temporary paralysis. I was going to use that to get away but in my panic had clawed at his gills. I don't think he's gonna hesitate next time. We resumed our circle.

Why did he hesitate? He could have ended it right there, so why?

I blinked and realized I was crying. I wiped away a tear, did seeing me cry make him stop? The other Síren lunged at me. I flipped onto my back and slapped at him.

✦ *Echo.* ✦

I looped around the other Síren's tail and grabbed onto her but she slipped away easily. I looked down at my hands, my fingers were too stiff to get a good grip. Well if I can't use my hands then I'll have to use my teeth. Watching each other, I noticed she seemed nervous. Her sail kept flicking up and down as if she couldn't decide if she was trying to be threatening or harmless. I smirked and swished my tail. Indecisiveness is good, I can use that.

The second I got a chance, I tried to sink my teeth into her, she in response grabbed my arm and attempted to twist it. I growled, and yanked my arm away.

◇ *Sáo.* ◇

If I keep going on the defence, then eventually the other Síren's going to break through. I'm barely blocking his attacks. I flicked my tail back and forth.

I struck again, aiming for his arms. He struggled to block my attacks. It seemed while the other Síren could attack with ease, defence was hard for him. I backed away for a moment, it makes sense that he can't defend very well. His arms were heavily injured. I shot towards the other Síren, striking at him. As I struck at him again I aimed for his side, specifically, the gashes on his side.

The other Síren screamed in pain as I deepened the gashes. He grabbed my arm and twisted it sharply. There was a loud popping sound and a sharp flash of pain rippled down my arm. I cried out in pain, and lashed at his shoulder while pulling away, while clutching my arm, I sensed him studying me, his gaze emotionless.

✦ *Echo.* ✦

I panted softly, it was getting hard to breathe and I was trying hard not to show that I was in pain. The other Síren had started being very offensive and it was hard to keep up. My gills flared open as wide as they could, trying to suck in as much water as possible. What should I do? Using my

141

arm-fins as shields like I usually did won't work, and my tail wasn't an option either. The little pest kept targeting the gashes on my side. I coughed, and glowered at her.

◇ *Sáo.* ◇

I hesitated, something about the other Síren seemed strangely familiar. Something in the way he glared at me. I shook my head. Impossible, the only Síren I knew were Moonhunter, Echo, and Frostsight. But Moonhunter has grey scales, Echo is dead, and Mum wasn't brought to Earth.

The other Síren hit me with a tail whip which was clearly painful for him. I dodged and moved closer, striking again at the gash on his left side. He shrieked in pain and lashed back at me. I dodged the attack and backed away slightly to think. Suddenly the other Síren swam right at me, and looped around me.

His tail wrapped around my chest and injured arm. Before I could react, he began to squeeze. I shrieked and started thrashing, but it didn't deter him, he only squeezed tighter. It felt familiar for some reason. I thought, feeling my ribs start to crack under the pressure.

A memory appeared in my mind. Me and Echo hunting walruses, Echo had done this weird attack that involved wrapping her tail around the walrus then punching its head.

Wait. I ducked, just in time as the other Síren's fist swung right where my head had been a second ago.

I turned my head to look back at him. Solid black scales on dark gray skin, blue frill and sail, he looked a lot like Echo. I quickly reached up, grabbing hold of the other Síren's left frill. I pinched down hard on the middle spine, he spasmed and released me. I darted away, clutching at my chest, my dislocated arm hanging at my side. I rubbed my chest, wincing when my fingers touched my bruised ribs. I watched the other Síren as he slowly regained control of his body. I cringed at myself, using pressure points didn't seem like a very fair way to fight especially since the other Síren was injured. I shook my head. I need to stop thinking about that, I just need to fight and win, that's all.

The other Síren sounded very familiar which was strange and confusing since the only male Síren I'd known was Moonhunter, and he was mute. But his cries of pain also seemed a bit too high pitched for a male, had I been wrong, was the other Síren a male? I'd assumed it was a male because he was larger than me, but now I wasn't so sure. Maybe... Wild-born are larger than city-born, maybe the other Síren was a female wild-born. No, Echo was a wild-born and this Síren is bigger than she was. So maybe a male wild-born?

✦ *Echo.* ✦

Rubbing my now sore frill, I watched the other Síren. Despite her obvious advantage she seemed hesitant. Attacking me, but now backing off for some reason. Sure I was retreating as well but that was out of defence. I wiggled my frill, debating between asking or just ignoring my curiosity. Curiosity won.

"You seem hesitant to fight me. Why?" I asked as we once again circled.

The other Síren blinked, she looked startled to hear me speak, her sail still twitched up and down. "You're hurt. It doesn't feel fair."

I snorted, flaring out my frill. "Fair? We're all hurt here. It's just the way it is."

She looked surprised at what I said. "It shouldn't

143

have to be," she whispered.

I huffed, "Well it is. There's nothing you can do to change that."

The other Síren flared out her frill, she looked a bit hurt by my reply. "That's nice. Are all male wild-born this depressing or is it just you?"

I paused for a moment trying to process what she said. "Male?...why you!" I bristled in outrage. "Male?! I'm a female!" I lunged at the offending Síren.

Her frill dropped. "Wait! I'm sorry I didn't mean to offend you!" she cried, darting from my attack. I screeched in response, and attempted to strike her again. But despite my burst of anger filled energy, I was still suffering from multiple injuries, including my torn gills. I slowed my chase, placing a hand over my gills and gasping softly. I could feel the other Síren watching me, I glared at her.

✧ *Sáo.* ✧

I watched the other Síren. Don't get your hopes up, Echo's dead you know she's dead, you saw her die. The other Síren's snarled words echoed through my head, but it wasn't the cruelty of what she said that brought me to tears. It was the fact that it was *Echo's* voice.

I looked over the other Síren with a more careful eye, fortunately –or unfortunately depending how you looked at it– since she was currently clutching at her gills struggling to breathe, she also wasn't attacking me.

She had the inward scalloped sail that I loved to run my fingers down because it felt funny, the absurdly long tail that gave her the sheer power and speed that only another wild-born could match. I tackled the other Síren, staring deep into her eyes. They were the same shade of ice blue.

144

Echo.

Although, I squinted at her. Her eye orbs seemed smaller and there was a strange ring of dark silver around them.

The sweet smell of blood tickled my nose, Echo was bleeding from the gashes in her sides. She growled at me, blood swirling out of her gills. Echo shoved me away. It's like my dream, I need to stop her.

"Echo! Echo it's Sáo!" I reached to pull her back, but Echo grasped at my arms and pinned me. She's not listening, stubborn wild-born. I paused, realizing something. Echo had changed, she was thinner. The Síren that had once been roughly two hundred pounds of "solid muscle and rage" as Echo herself had once joked, was now so thin, I could faintly see her ribs. If she's changed this much in such a short time, how much have I changed?

I wiggled, Echo's grip seemed weak and her hands felt strange, like sea serpent leather. Even with my dislocated shoulder I had the superior grip. I grabbed her by the shoulders and flipped us over.

Pinning her down on her back with my non-dislocated arm, I managed to put my other forearm right in front of her nose.

"Look Echo! Look at the scales!" Echo snarled and thrashed but while I had her on her back she couldn't do much. "Echo, please look at me." Echo growled and sank her teeth in my dislocated arm. I tried not to scream. I really should've seen that coming.

"Ow. Ow. Ow. Ow." I moved my arm to a position where Echo had no choice but to look me in the eye. "Echo… it's me." Echo's frill flared out and she snarled at me.

She doesn't recognize me. I paused, I need to do something so unbelievably me, that it's obvious.

"Look!" I stopped pinning her with my non-injured arm and pointed at my eyes, "Eye orbs!" Echo went still, her frill lowered, she stared up at me.

✦ *Echo.* ✦

I blinked once. Eye orbs? A memory flickered through my mind.

"Look! See? Eye orbs!" Shimmering water. Sáo, pointing at her eyes. Smiling at me like she always did. Her pale green eyes glinting with that same amusement she had when she was teaching me something new.

I blinked up at the Síren pinning me down. Pure white scales, that short, outward scalloped sail, the arm-fins with a dozen holes in the edges from her biting them, and the dark gray scales scattered across her forearms.

My frill flicked forward, "Pffffft." I rolled onto my side, shaking with laughter as she floated off me. "Eye orbs! Ha!"

Sáo snorted softly, "I don't see what's so funny."

I wiped a tear off my face. "Nothing. It-" I hesitated, looking at her.

The very first friend I had, the Síren who I thought was dead. I lunged at her, catching Sáo off guard. Grabbing her, I pulled her into a hug. Sáo went still.

"I thought you didn't like hugs," she murmured, hugging me back.

"Oh, go lick a rock. You're ruining the moment," I grumbled.

✧ *Sáo.* ✧

I smiled, "And I hate to ruin it further but we have to keep

146

fighting."

Echo pulled away slightly. "Why?"

I wiggled out of her hug a bit more. "I'll tell you in a minute, right now I need you to hit me." Echo just seemed more confused but she complied, sending me tumbling backward. When I stopped spinning I lunged forward and I mock slashed her across the chest.

"We have to fight, if we don't the humans will kill us."

Echo glanced up at the pit's edge before she slapped me with her tail sending me spinning. "Then what do we do? Eventually they're going to notice we're not actually fighting."

I lunged at Echo and bit her sail. Echo cried out in pain and lashed at me. I quickly darted away and spit the piece of sail out of my mouth. "Bleh, ice slabs lied to me. Síren sail does not taste like frosted slither-fish."

Echo shook herself. "First, ow. Second, what?"

"Uh… nothing."

Echo eyed me suspiciously, then launched herself at me in a hug. "What are you doing? I asked, enjoying the hug but nervous that the humans might notice. Echo chuckled and bit my shoulder, hard. "Just checking."

I hissed, and zipped away. Echo cackled and followed me, although I noticed she was moving slower than before. I slowed down a little to give her a chance to catch up.

"Is there any way we can get out of this?" Echo asked, dodging my attack that she somehow saw coming.

I shook my head. "I don't think so." I gave a mock charge which Echo dodged. Echo slashed at me as I passed her.

"Well I suppose there is one way," I mused, attempting to dodge Echo's slash.

"And what way would that be?" Echo asked, as she ever so calmly removed a piece of my sail.

"Well, it's a terrible idea but one of us could theoretically sacrifice themself so the other would survive."

Echo hesitated slightly, "and you're offering yourself?"

I huffed, and smacked her. "Well I don't hear you making any offers."

"Sáo, in the entire year I lived with you I've heard all sorts of horrible ideas." She grabbed my shoulders and took a deep breath. "BUT THAT IS THE WORST IDEA THAT HAS EVER COME OUT OF YOUR MOUTH." She yelled, shaking me viciously.

"Ok! Ok! It was horrible! I'm sorry!"

Echo stopped shaking me, "Good, now." She grinned evilly and grabbed me by the tail-fin, before throwing me into a pit wall.

I slammed into the wall, fortunately Echo hadn't thrown me too hard. Think about it, I saw Echo hit by that explosion and naturally thought she died. I pictured it, the loud bang, Echo spasming in the water once before going still, her purple blood spilling out into the water. I shivered, the last thing I wanted was to see Echo die again. While I don't know what Echo saw she probably doesn't want to see me dead either.

I glanced up at where the humans were then back at Echo. She was definitely moving slower now as well as gasping softly with each breath. She's going to die, even if the humans don't kill her, even if I don't kill her. She'll die anyway. Her injuries are beyond what I know how to handle. I don't even know what she fought, much less how to treat her.

"One of us could pretend to be dead," I offered.

Echo shook her head and coughed, "We don't know what the humans will do with us once we're dead."

"Yeah, you're right."

I looped around Echo, pulling her into a choke hold. "Hold still, I'm going to see if I can do something about those damaged gills of yours." Echo coughed again but didn't struggle.

✦ *Echo.* ✦

Suddenly there was a loud rumbling sound. Sáo released me from the choke hold and we both looked around nervously, the water rippling.

"What was that?" Sáo asked. I warily peeked my head out of the water as far as I could, I didn't dare try to climb the pit wall. From my limited angle I could just barely see humans running all around the pit. They were screaming and panicking, and there were loud bangs coming from somewhere just out of my line of view.

I looked around, it was hard to see anything outside the pit. All of the humans running around didn't help either. I squinted, I didn't recognize anyone I saw. Except for one, the muscular human. It was standing fairly close to the pit, yelling and pointing something smallish and black at something just out of my line of view.

There was a loud crackling noise and a burst of fire erupted from where the muscular human was looking. The fire enveloped it and the human's angry yells turned into screams of pain and terror. It collapsed, disappearing from view as another human walked up to the pit taking it's place.

The new human stared at us for a moment before turning to call out to something and moving away. Sáo swam up next to me as I sank back beneath the water. "What's happening up there?" she asked. I shook my head, "I don't know."

We both stared up at the edge of the pit waiting, after a few minutes we stopped seeing humans run by the pit, the banging and fire stopped, it was quiet.

A human suddenly appeared at the pit's edge, it chattered to something before sliding down into the pit. I hissed and raised my sail. The human approached slowly, lifting its hands. I watched it move closer, the water was at the human's chest. Human's can't move very well in water, I realized, watching the human struggle to approach. It got just within two tail lengths from us, and to our surprise it began to speak in a strange garbling voice. It took a minute but I started to understand what it was saying.

"It's ok, I'm not gonna hurt you," it murmured. "I'm part of the SPF. We're here to help."

✦ *Chapter 12* ✦

✦ *Echo.* ✦

I stretched and repositioned myself. The container I was in was quite nice, much nicer than the ones the humans had put me in before. This container was larger with little 'windows' for me to look out. I stretched my tail out once again. There was a soft tapping sound above my head. I glanced up, it was one of the SPF humans who was moving me. I believe his name was Fen, to my knowledge he was a male human.

Fen lifted the clear top of the container. "We'll be there in about twenty minutes. Are you doing alright? I know you've got claustrophobia."

"Yeah. I'm alright, the windows help."

Just past Fen I could hear Sáo talking to another human. She was asking how the humans were moving us so easily. Apparently the humans had cast a 'feather-weight spell' on the containers so that they could carry us. Sáo seemed to find that fascinating and kept asking more questions about how the spell worked.

Fen grinned, "Your friend is very curious about our spells. Been asking questions the whole ride." I thought about that and cringed.

"Sorry about that," I said, also having been a victim

of Sáo's curiosity.

Fen grinned harder, "No worries. I'm not one of her caretakers, so I'm safe." Fen glanced back over where Sáo's container was. "Welp, I should probably go help Aril get out of that conversation now. She's been staring daggers at me for the past couple minutes and if I don't go she might think I'm purposely ignoring her."

I swished my tail, "Have you? Been purposely ignoring her?"

Fen gasped and placed a hand to his chest, "I would never,"he said before closing the lid. I coiled up and chuckled to myself. Humans helping us, imagine that. If someone had told me two weeks ago that a group of humans were going to save me from the other humans, fix me up, and then bring me back to the ocean. I shook my head, I definitely wouldn't have believed them. I thought back to just over a week ago.

The human that had jumped into the pit with us was the first nice human we'd met. It stayed there with us for a while, explaining that it was there to help and what was gonna happen.

After a blur of events the SPF humans had us in large containers. They brought us to a new place that reminded me of where I'd lived with Tulva except much bigger. After a week or so of 'rehabilitation' as the humans called it, the SPF decided that we were healthy enough to be released.

Now they were bringing us both back to the ocean, using large containers with little clear spots so we could look out. Nothing like the containers the other humans used. They were also using something called a 'truck' to carry us for the journey.

While we were living at the rehabilitation center, we learned that it was Larissa and Squishy who tracked us down. They had been at the rehabilitation center too for a little while but since Larissa and Squishy didn't have any extreme injuries they were already brought back to the ocean. Apparently they were waiting for Sáo and I.

I closed my eyes, thinking about the ocean. Tap, tap. I blinked, it was Sáo in her separate container.

She waved at me and mouthed something, "You good?"

I offered her a little smile in return and nodded.

She smiled, "Me too," she mouthed back. I closed my eyes again and dozed off. I woke up a bit later when I felt my container being sharply jostled.

I peered out through one of the windows. Some SPF humans –and no, despite having lived with them for a week neither Sáo nor I knew what SFP meant– were now carrying my container.

I swam in a circle. "What's happening?" I called.

Fen appeared over my container, "Sorry, forgot to warn you. We just unloaded you from the truck, that's all."

"Oh, ok," I said, a bit confused about what that meant.

Fen sat down in front of one of the windows.

"Shouldn't you be helping the others?" I asked.

Fen gave me a pained grin, "Just rolled my ankle so I'm resting to take the weight off it for a few minutes, I'm useless at healing spells."

"Does…it hurt?" I asked, unsure what to say.

"It's basically the human equivalent of twisting a tail-fin," He replied.

I winced in sympathy, I'd done that many times as a youngling so I knew how much it could hurt.

"So, how's this gonna work? You're gonna carry the container to the ocean and then what?" I asked, suddenly feeling awkward.

Fen adjusted the way he was sitting, "Simple. We

153

open the door to the container and you'll just slide on out."

"Door? I thought you were just gonna use that web again and lift me out."

"You mean the sling? Well, we would. But the container's too tall to do that without ladders and the ground near the ocean is pretty uneven and soft, so using ladders is dangerous."

"So then where's the door?" I asked.

"Well, it's not really a door, what happens is one of us casts a spell and the glass from this window–" he tapped the largest window "–opens up."

I eyed the window warily, Fen chuckled.

"Don't worry, it won't disappear right now. Someone has to cast the spell first."

Just then another human appeared near Fen, "Oh already? Ok."

"What's happening now?" I asked, but Fen just gave me a 'thumbs up' and moved out of my view. I felt the SPF humans pick up my container again, I watched through the windows as they brought me over to what looked to be the ocean.

The container was now facing forward so I could see the ocean through the big window.

"Here you go!" Fen said. I heard one of the humans say something in a strange language and suddenly the big window disappeared.

Fen lied, I did not 'slide out.' When the window disappeared, all of the water rushed out dragging me with it. I squealed in terror the entire time, I felt like a youngling trying to swim in a current for the first time.

Having just seen my life flash before my eyes, I laid on the ocean floor for a moment resting. Hearing a familiar voice call my name I swam to the surface. It was Fen.

"Well? Wasn't that fun?" Fen asked, crouching down to talk to me. Cupping my hand I flung water at him.

"Fun? That was terrifying!" I shrieked.

Fen wiped his face, "Ah well, I guess it's not everyone's thing."

I huffed and looked around, we were in a small bay-like area which connected to a larger bay. The water was rather shallow, only about two tail-lengths where I was but dropped off where the two bays connected. I glanced back, the SPF humans were pulling my container away and went to get Sáo's container. From what I could tell, Aril was ordering Fen to help.

There was a loud whinny and I was suddenly tackled from the side, I whipped around ready to defend myself. It was a largish dark blue and white creature that was currently nuzzling my head. "Hello to you too, Larissa," I laughed while petting her.

Suddenly, without any warning Larissa nipped me sharply in the frill. I pulled back and rubbed my frill, she'd bit it hard enough to draw blood.

"She says that was for disappearing and nearly giving her a panic attack," a voice said.

I looked around for the speaker. The speaker was a smallish human sitting on an outcropping rock nearby.

It grinned, "Hi, I'm Dei. I helped Squishy and Larissa find you."

I eyed the small human warily, Larissa neighed something to the human who shook its head.

"No, I can't. I'm grounded. No basic spell casting for two weeks and no big spells for a month. Aril said that if she spots me even thinking about casting a spell she'll full on deck me. I don't know if she was joking or not and I don't really want to find out."

155

One of the humans who was carrying Sáo's container closer to the water promptly yelled, "I'll do it! Screw what Abÿss and Cámi said. I'll do it!"

I looked over at the yelling human, it was Aril, who looked after Sáo. Fen often spoke about Aril. I'd always thought that Aril seemed nice, she seemed very excitable. While I knew nothing about romance I had a feeling Fen and Aril were courting.

I waited patiently for the humans to release Sáo from her container. She looked around, getting her bearings. When she spotted me, she darted over.

"Echo, Echo, Echo!" she cried, crushing my ribs in a one-armed hug.

"That's my name," I said mildly amused. Noticing how excited Sáo was, I wiggled slightly trying to get out of her grasp.

"Did you know that all of the SPF humans we've met aren't actually humans?" Sáo began shaking me, hard. "They aren't human, they're actually hybrids! Human/Elf hybrids! That's how they can do magic! Isn't that cool?! They even used magic to move us! They cast a 'feather-weight spell' to make the containers we were in easier to carry. It meant they could avoid having to use this thing called a 'crane.'" She stopped shaking me only to spin the two of us around in a circle. "I don't know what a crane is but it sounds cool, right?!"

Fortunately for me, as easy as Sáo was to excite, she was equally easy to distract. Suddenly, spotting her pet kraken Sáo darted off with a cry, "Squishy!"

I flopped backward in the water, my head spinning.

"Uh, is she alright?" Dei asked.

"Is who alright? Oh, oops. Sorry Echo," Sáo apologized.

"I'm fine. Just gonna –ah– lie here for a bit. At least you didn't throw me into a rock this time," I replied.

"Oh come on! That was an accident!"

"An accident my head still remembers."

Sáo turned away from me and began cooing to Squishy again.

"He says he's glad you're alright," Dei said.

Sáo looked over at him. "You can understand what Squishy's saying?"

The little human nodded. "Yup! I've got a translator spell on him right now." Dei then winced, "Well actually Cámi had to cast the spell for me but I can still understand him."

I stared up at the stars, only half listening to their conversation. Sáo was drilling Dei about spells, something she seemed very interested in so she'd most likely tell me everything she learned later.

Larissa nudged my side.

"I'm fine," I said, patting her head.

Larissa neighed at me.

"I said I'm fine, look, see?" I rolled over so I wasn't on my back anymore. "Perfectly fine."

Larissa eyed me for a second, making me feel like I was being judged then neighed at Dei.

"She'll know," Dei replied. Larissa neighed again, more forcefully.

"What does she want?" I asked, running my finger through her mane.

"Oh, she wants me to cast a translator spell so that you'll be able to understand her and Squishy. But like I said, I'm grounded, no spells." Larissa moved closer, pulling herself onto the rock, and rested her head on the little human's lap.

The two stared at each other for about a minute before Dei muttered a quiet "Fine." Larissa backed away, bobbing her head up and down in excitement. Dei glanced around quickly while Sáo and I watched curiously. Then the human closed its eyes and started muttering too quickly for me to understand.

Suddenly there were several quick steps and Aril appeared out of nowhere and tackled Dei, knocking them both into the water. I tilted my head, barely a minute later Aril resurfaced dragging Dei with it. Aril dumped Dei back on the rock with a "Told you I'd do it." Before going back to help the other humans.

Dei coughed, and sat up. Larissa chuffed softly. "Don't laugh at me. This is your fault," he grumbled. "Now I'm cold and wet, my least favorite things." Larissa chuffed louder.

Then I noticed another container being hauled out. It was rattling slightly and the humans kept talking to whatever was inside it. I shrugged and turned my attention to a rather annoyed Larissa who was now gnawing on my sail. There was an angry shrieking noise and the glass in the front window of the third container vanished.

A Síren tumbled out, hissing with his sail raised. Sáo cried out in alarm and backed away. Stopping my attempts to separate Larissa from my sail, I glanced over at the other Síren.

"Oh, it's you."

He turned towards me. *I recognize that voice.*

"You had the audacity to forget?"

You know, I thought I was finally free of you when those humans came but no, you had to come back and haunt me again.

"I was just thinking the exact same thing," I growled.

158

I can think of one good thing though. He sounded quite pleased.

"Oh? And what's that?" I drawled.

Now that I can't see, I don't have to suffer with looking at you anymore.

I blinked trying to understand what he said. Then it occurred to me that his eyes were dull and gray. "Why you..."

Sáo watched me and Moonhunter argue for several minutes before interrupting. "Sorry to interrupt this very fascinating argument. But uh, who on Neptune is he?!"

Moonhunter jumped away, *who said that?!*

Sáo squinted at him, "Oh wait now I recognize you, you're that Síren from the tank."

What?

"Oh yeah, I never introduced myself back then. Sorry. I'm Sáo, daughter of Frostsight and Flickertail. You are?"

Moonhunter froze in place, I could see him analyzing what she said. He grabbed Sáo and pulled her closer to him, gently tracing her sail, frill, and cheeks.

"Uhhh, help," Sáo said, trying to pull away from Moonhunter who was now desperately hugging her.

"Oh right, I suppose I never told you." I cleared my throat and gestured at the male city-born, "Sáo, this is your older brother Moonhunter. You conveniently left out how much of a pain he is when telling me about him."

Sáo blinked at me, "Moonhunter. My older brother Moonhunter?"

Yes.

Sáo grabbed Moonhunter's face and examined it. She gasped softly, "It is you!" Somehow even though Moonhunter was already hugging her, Sáo tackled him back.

I watched them sibling bond for a few seconds before

deciding to ruin the moment.

"I gotta say, I'm surprised. I thought the humans finally got you," I drawled.

Moonhunter lashed his tail instantly aggravated, *you wish.*

One of the humans approached us, I turned to face it. "I know Síren are territorial creatures but do you think you and Sáo could… look after Moonhunter? Unfortunately the damage to his eyes is permanent, he will never be able to see again. If you don't want to look out for him, that's ok but we won't be able to release him," it said.

"Sure!" Sáo said, still hugging Moonhunter.

"Nope," I replied exactly at the same time. Sáo and I turned to stare at each other.

Moonhunter wiggled out of his sister's grasp. *I don't see the point of this. I can take care of myself.*

"You can't see anything," I shot back.

Moonhunter glared at me, or well he tried to. He ended up scowling at a rather frightened Dei instead of me.

"Wrong direction. I'm over here, which just proves my point."

Sáo grasped my arm and stared up at me. "Please? He's my brother."

I don't need help.

I gestured at Moonhunter, "See he's fine. The humans will look after him. It'll be safer for him with the humans."

Sáo's eyes began to water.

"No, stop."

A tear ran down.

"Stop it. That's not gonna work."

Another tear, "Please?"

I narrowed my eyes. "No. it's not- he isn't- stop that." We stared each other down.

160

-✦-

I grumply led the way back to the cave, Sáo followed close behind me tightly holding the hand of a both smug and annoyed Moonhunter. Larissa swam beside me and Squishy was somewhere on the ocean floor. It took several hours but we arrived at the cave with no incident or human sightings.

Sáo brought Moonhunter over to a large rock and settled him there. Moonhunter warily felt around the rock.

"Stay there, I'm gonna make you a bed in a minute," Sáo said before leaving, with Larissa following her. Moonhunter nodded, he stayed on the rock for maybe two minutes before bravely creeping off.

I coiled up on my bed and watched him, he wandered near where Squishy was rock stacking but quickly retreated when Squishy flicked him on the nose for getting too close. Moonhunter then began wandering my way, he batted at my bed several times before seeming to realize what it was. Patting at my bed he slowly moved closer, when he was barely half a tail-length from me I suddenly grabbed his arm.

"Boo," I said.

Moonhunter gave a raspy shriek and darted back to the rock where Sáo left him. He sat there, coiled up his sail and frill flattened. *Don't do that.*

I blinked, surprised that he'd been so frightened, "Sorry."

We descended into an awkward silence, the only sound was that of Squishy continuing to stack rocks. Fortunately we were saved by Sáo reappearing in the cave entrance holding a woven bed.

Sáo placed the bed near Moonhunter, "There, that's your bed."

Moonhunter awkwardly felt at his new bed. Sáo tilted her head, "Is something wrong?"

No, it's just very large.

Sáo laughed. "Oh yeah, I had to get used to that too. Turns out wild-born have these really big beds because they're not worried about space in the den."

But then you'd risk food getting in your bed if it's bigger.

I huffed, "Use your brain –if you even have one– no eating allowed in the cave. Basic rule."

Moonhunter picked up a stone and threw it in my general direction. Unfortunately Sáo was also in my general direction. I struggled not to laugh as the resulting chaos ensued.

✦ *Far, far away. On a certain Síren inhabited planet.* ✦

Gillcutter sat quietly on a large rock, staring out into the open ocean. The water next to him shifted and a very large Síren settled onto the rock with him. He didn't need to turn around to know who it was.

"Greetings, Mother."

Hello, youngling.

Gillcutter shook his head, the Great Mother referred to all Síren as younglings. "What's the reason for this particular visit?"

The Great Mother was quiet for a minute. *Your daughter.*

"Hm. What of her?"

She is on Earth now.

Gillcutter went quiet. "Is she-"

No, she is still alive. She is too far away for me to communicate with her, or see what she is doing. But I can still feel her, I know she is alright.

"If she's still alive then that means she's nearly old enough for a mate now."

Yes. You did it, you got another youngling to adulthood. How many is that now?

"Why do you ask? You already know."

Yes, tell me about each of them.

Gillcutter sighed. "The first was Háli, he was very independent and strong. I was not surprised when you brought news of his success. The second was Icefall, her mother named her but I raised her. She enjoyed teasing her older brother. The third and fourth were the twins Nereid and Neso. I was shocked when you said that Neso had made it, he was quite small and fragile for a wild-born. Unlike his twin, who seemed to have absorbed all of his brother's strength and size."

Gillcutter shifted positions, "And now Echo."

And now Echo, that makes five. The Great Mother smiled, *five younglings to make it to adulthood. That is a good number.*

Gillcutter tried not to laugh, "And how many have you seen to adulthood?" he asked.

A number far too large for your mind to handle.

Gillcutter was about to ask more– about what he wasn't sure when the Great Mother interrupted him.

Shh, listen.

Gillhunter pricked up his frill. Just faintly over the sound of the currents, he could hear a familiar voice calling his name. He turned in a circle looking for the source, there.

Another Síren, with scales of blue and dark gray, swimming along the border of his territory. He smiled, had it been any other Síren, he would've already chased them off. But not this one, no, this one he would follow to the edges of Neptune if she wished him to. Gillhunter suddenly felt his sail prickle and turned back to the Great Mother. She was smiling at him.

What are you waiting for? Your mate is calling.

Gillcutter swam out to the other Síren, "Thalassa!" he called.

The other Síren turned at the sound of his voice and shrieked in excitement. The two swam in a spiraling dance for a little while and when Gillcutter glanced back at where he'd left the Great Mother, she was gone. Gillcutter blinked. For a Síren as large as her, she moves fast.

Thalassa ruffled his frill, "Looking for someone? Say. How are the younglings? They should be out territory hunting by now."

Gillcutter smiled at her. "Only one hatched, you would've liked her. Her name was Echo."

✦ *Tulva.* ✦

Tulva swam around his pool, going in his customary circle. The aquarium had been so boring since Echo left. He looked up out of the water at the stars. I hope Echo made it back to the ocean and found her pod again. He thought.

Tulva blinked, some of the stars seemed to be falling, they were approaching him. The stars swirled together forming what looked to be an orca.

<Hello Tulva.> The orca said.

Tulva backed away slightly. <Who are you?> He asked, a bit worried.

The other orca clicked softly, <don't you recognize me?>

Tulva examined the starry orca, she felt strangely familiar to him but he hadn't seen another orca since- Tulva's

164

eyes widened, <Mama?>

The star orca swam closer and nuzzled him.

<I thought you were gone.> He said.

<I was.> The starry orca swam up above Tulva's pool, <follow me, Tulva. To the Eternal Ocean.>

As Tulva began swimming up to his mom he felt his body changing, growing lighter. He swam up to the starry orca and realized he was now made up of stars too. Tulva knew about the Eternal Ocean of course, all orcas knew about it. All dolphins, porpoises, and whales knew about it too. When he had been a calf, his pod would tell him about the Eternal Ocean.

When Tulva caught up to her, his mom turned and kept going up towards the stars. He followed for a little while then stopped, the starry orca turned around.

<What's wrong?> She asked, concerned.

<I'm not ready.>

<You wish to see that friend of yours,> His mom said.

<Yes.>

The starry orca didn't look surprised. <I had a feeling you'd want to see her again. Come I know where she is.>

They swam through the sky for a while before approaching the ocean, they swooped down to a little cove. As they swam over the cove Tulva spotted Echo, she was talking with two other Síren. While he didn't recognize one of them, he knew the other, Moonhunter.

Tulva whistled happily, Echo had found her pod. He was tempted to call to her then realized.

<She can't see or hear me can she?> Tulva said.

<She can't,> His mom replied.

Tulva watched the group until Echo and the others disappeared under the water. <Are you ready now?> The

165

starry orca asked.

Tulva nodded, he was ready. The starry orca began swimming straight upward towards the sky. After a moment's hesitation Tulva followed. As he swam higher and higher, more of his former pod joined him. His aunts, uncles, cousins, brothers, and sisters were all swimming with him.

Going up to the Eternal Ocean, where Tulva knew he'd never have to worry about being caught by a human ever again.

✦ *Echo.* ✦

I stared out at the open ocean. Sáo and Moonhunter were asleep, after the whole Moonhunter-threw-a-rock-at-Sáo incident. Sáo decided we were all just cranky from an entire day of the SPF humans taking us to the ocean and that we needed rest. Apparently Sáo was really tired because she fell asleep within a few minutes, Moonhunter dozed off shortly after.

That was several hours ago, I was still awake. A short swim might help. I glanced back at the others, they wouldn't notice. I swam out of the cave and began going up. I kept swimming up until I reached my destination: the surface.

Floating, I rolled onto my back and stared up at the night sky. Or whatever counted as night on this sun-bright planet. As I watched the stars and moon, I tried looking for Neptune. Pretty pointless since Neptune was too far away to be seen, but I did it anyway, occasionally swishing my tail or paddling my arms to keep from drifting away.

Staring up at a spot where I thought Neptune might be, I wondered why we were sent here. I never really questioned it before, why were three Wanderlings stolen away and sent to Earth? I thought with a yawn. I shook my head. No, can't be just us three, there must be more Síren on Earth than that.

I yawned again. Guess the stargazing worked, now I'm tired.

I flipped right side up and began the descent back to the cave. I am quite curious now. Why *were* we sent here? I wondered if the others knew since they were city-born. Sáo most likely doesn't know, she would've told me by now if she did. Hard to guess if Moonhunter knows, he seems like the kind of Síren who keeps track of stuff like that. I arrived at the cave and quickly checked to see if my absence was noticed. The others were still asleep, although Squishy was wide awake and staring at me accusingly with his massive eyes. I motioned for him to stay quiet and scooted to my nest.

I curled up, adjusting the seaweed leaves for maximum comfiness. Well if none of us knew why we were sent to Earth, maybe there's another Síren on Earth that does. I closed my eyes. We'll just have to find them.

Síren terms translated.

Hatchling: The Síren equivalent of a human toddler.
Youngling: The Síren equivalent of a human child to early teen, (ages 5 to 14.)
Wanderling: The Síren equivalent of a human late teen to young adult, (ages 15 to 20.)
Adult: The Síren equivalent of a human adult.
Elder: The Síren equivalent of a human senior, (ages 65 to 100.)
No, I did not have to translate those last two. But I did it anyway.

Frill: Three spines with webbing between them on both sides of the head. Webbing can be outwardly scalloped, inwardly scalloped, or smooth. Not only positioned and functional like ears, the spines in the frill allow Síren to move in different directions. It is often used for expressing emotion.

Sail: Similar to the frill it consists of a series of spines with webbing between. Webbing can be outwardly scalloped, inwardly scalloped, or smooth. Starting at the top of the forehead and stretching down the back continuing down the tail ending at the tail-fin. Unlike the frill it is only capable of up and down movement, used as a way of steering and for expressing emotion.

Arm-fins: Again like the previously mentioned, row of spines with webbing between. You know it's coming. Webbing can be outwardly scalloped, inwardly scalloped, or smooth. Starting at the wrist and ending at the elbow. Like the sail, arm-fins have limited movement. The arm-fins aren't really used for expressing emotion.

Glow-scales: A pattern of scales that grow once a wanderling matures into an adult. These scales are used to attract potential mates.

Open gills: A genetic mutation that causes the gills of the affected Síren to be wider. This mutation doesn't really have any drawbacks to it although a Síren with open gills may find that they are incapable of closing their gills and that they dry out quicker when above ice. This mutation allows for longer bursts of speed as the wider gills can suck in more water preventing loss of breath. It is predominantly found in wild-born but city-born can have it the odd time.

Great Mother: The ancestor of all Síren. She watches over, teaches, and guides her descendants through telepathy, sometimes even appearing in physical form. She is one of twelve Great Ancestors and one of two that dwell on Neptune.
Great Ancestor: The Ancestor of an intelligent supernatural species. Very powerful, and presumably immortal.

Wild-born: A subspecies of Síren, closely related to the city-born. They tend to be larger, more aggressive and territorial. Wild-born are also stronger and have more stamina as they are built to travel long distances.
City-born: A subspecies of Síren, closely related to wild-born. They tend to be smaller, less aggressive, and will share

territory. What the city-born are lacking in power they have in agility and speed over short distances.

Kraken: A large octopus, native to Neptune.
Sea Serpent: A water-dwelling snake, native to Neptune.
Slither- ish: An eel-like fish, native to Neptune.
Hippocampus: A half horse-half fish creature, native to Neptune.
Kelpie: A carnivorous horse made entirely of water, native to Neptune.

Glow Shroom: A massive glowing mushroom found only in Neptune.
Seaweed: If you don't know what seaweed is then I don't know what to say.

-✦-

Gill-rot: A semi-contagious, often fatal illness that infects the gills. The fatal part is more common with wild-born as they live a more dangerous lifestyle. Gill-rot is more common among Síren with open gills as the bacteria can easier enter the wider gills. Gill-rot can be caused by being bitten by an infected Purfin, eating a rotten corpse –even Síren have to resort to scavenging sometimes– swimming too close to a volcano, or swimming in a kraken brooding pit. Although with that last one it's not really the pit itself that causes it, but the female kraken inside heating the water for their eggs so really it is swimming in warm water for long periods of time that can cause gill-rot. Good thing the only planets with lots of water hot enough for gill-rot causing bacteria to thrive are Earth and Satern, two planets Síren are not native to right?

Tail-length: Translates to roughly five feet. I bet you thought it was smaller than that, didn't you?

Neptunian year: About 165 Earth years. Echo and Sáo lived on Earth for a Neptunian year undisturbed before getting captured.

Ice-slab: A literal, inch thick, slab of ice with writing carved into it. They are the Síren version of a book because they don't have paper, or well, part of a book at least. For an entire book you'd need several ice-slabs. As an entire story cannot be told on just one so several will be kept in a pouch made of sea serpent leather together to keep them in order, and from getting scratched.

Vampire: A polar bear like supernatural that lives above the ice on Neptune. They speak via telepathy as the way their mouths are designed makes them incapable of speech.

Tassta: The Vampire home city, and only Vampire city.

Component: An object used in a spell. A component can be anything from a Dragon's eye, to a very normal, very unmagical sock, fresh from the dryer.

Seeking spell: Used to find lost objects or missing people.

Can be basic or advanced depending on the use. For a lost object all that is needed is something similar to the lost thing. Example: a sock –everybody's lost a sock at some point– all you need is the other sock to the pair. For a person you'd need something they'd touched recently, oftentimes with a missing person multiple seeking spells must be cast.

Sensory spell: Enhances one or more of the five senses. Dei used this spell to enhance Larissa's sense of smell.

Camouflage spell: Advanced spell, casting it with different components results in different kinds of camouflage.

Healing spell: Kind of self explanatory isn't it.

Feather-weight spell: Makes an object of choice lighter. It took the spells of thirteen members of the SPF to make just Echo's container light enough for ten people to carry. Even then the container was still pretty heavy.

Floating thing: This is a boat. Yup, just a boat. Nothin' fancy.
Web: Usually when mentioned this is a net or a sling used for transporting whales.

About Author

Do people actually read these? Oh shoot, someone's reading it.

Chaos Mage lives somewhere in the great white North, Canada. She spends most of her time hibernating indoors, and being an unsociable introvert. Definitely because of all the snow, yes, definitely the snow. Every once in a while, Chaos braves the scary outdoors and activates her magpie senses. She wanders around gathering tiny shiny things. Her fascination with small objects could be considered a problem by some. *cough, cough* *her mother*.

Chaos enjoys reading, writing, art, playing video games, and reading. She often gets new ideas for writing from whatever book/movie/show she's currently obsessed with, although Chaos has gotten inspiration from other sources too.

Chaos primarily focuses on writing, but also freelances as a graphic designer.

Were you waiting for more credentials? Chaos is [REDUCTED] years old and this is her first published book. Depending on how this goes, there *may* be a sequel. *Maybe.*

Manufactured by Amazon.ca
Bolton, ON

45587127R00104